STARLIGHT ACADEMY

D0239355

Dedication

To my mum, who has taught me what is important in life, with love and gratitude

RAGGED BEARS
Published by Ragged Bears Ltd.
The Granary
Compton Pauncefoot
Somerset BA22 7EL, UK

First published 2013

1 3 5 7 9 10 8 6 4 2

Text copyright © Jessica Renison, 2013
Illustrations copyright © Anne Claxton, 2013

The moral right of the author has been asserted

All rights reserved

A CIP catalogue record for this book is available from the British Library

ISBN 978-1-85714-421-5

Printed in Poland

www.ragged-bears.co.uk

STARLIGHT ACADEMY

Jess Renison

Ragged Bears

Contents

Chapter 1: *First Day*

Cassie tried not to look at the school as they drove up, because she didn't want to like it. But as she stared hard at her grazed knees she couldn't help noticing through the trees a huge sandy castle rising up into the spotless sky. Its high turrets were crawling with ivy, and it had cute fairytale windows which twinkled in the sunlight. So this was where she would be living for the next five years – or at least until she got brave enough to run away. She stretched her legs out and put her feet up on the dashboard of the car. She had natural dancer's legs, everyone said – just like her mother's apparently, though she'd never met her – but Cassie's were covered in scratches and bruises because really she preferred climbing trees to dancing.

They had been driving uphill through a thick forest and when they emerged at the top, the school stood before them in all its grandeur.

'So, what do you think?'

Her dad was trying to sound jolly when really she could tell that he was sad too. How would he manage without her? She tried not to think about it, but it was like trying not to press a bruise. An image came into her mind of him holding a piece of burnt toast with a puzzled look on his face, wondering how it had happened. She wanted to say, *I think it's crazy, me coming here*, but said instead, 'It looks nice.'

'It even has a real drawbridge,' said her dad in his best cheerful voice.

They had pulled up at an arched doorway with an ancient looking wooden door in it. Above the door there hung a silver metal flag with pretend folds in it. The words 'Starlight Academy' were carved across it in gold lettering. Next to it, there was a brass bell with a thick, red rope hanging down.

'We have to ring the bell here and someone will let the drawbridge down,' explained her dad. 'Do you want to get out and do it?'

She didn't, but she got out anyway.

The building they had stopped at was the gatehouse and the school lay beyond it. There was a real moat running around the edge of the school, just beyond the gatehouse.

They're certainly making sure it's difficult to escape from this place, thought Cassie, *but a stupid little moat won't stop me.*

She hadn't wanted to go to boarding school, but after bringing her up on his own for nine years since her mother died when she was two, Cassie's dad had decided that she needed more company, and perhaps a more feminine influence in her life.

'A few rules wouldn't hurt either,' he had added,

although as far as Cassie was concerned, she had got along just fine without any.

Cassie looked up at the fake waves in the stiff metal sign and sighed. She felt a deep sense of sadness about the flag, which should be flying freely in the wind but had been captured, frozen mid-flutter, never to move again. She had just reached up to pull the bell rope, when she heard a smash of crunching metal behind her and spun round to see that another car had crashed into the back of theirs. A woman with wild hair burst out of the car, her hands over her mouth in a gasp of horror.

'I'm *so* sorry! Oh gosh – look what I've done! I'm terribly, terribly stupid. I tried to stop but I was in such a rush and I just couldn't.'

'Don't worry. Not your fault at all.'

Cassie's dad was always so nice to people. He never got angry with anyone. Of course it was her fault!

'We're always late you see, and I was determined not to be late today of all days …'

Mr March glanced at his watch, 'You're not late.'

'Aren't we? How nice.'

Cassie looked through the window into the back seat of the other car. The front seat was full of papers and books, with a sleeping cat perched on top of the pile. The girl in the back rolled her eyes at Cassie and shook her head in despair. Then she smiled. For the first time that day, Cassie felt happy for a moment. It was like having a warm blanket wrapped around her after hours of shivering. But she didn't want to make friends here because she didn't want to like it here. She wasn't going to stay here. So she frowned and turned away. She opened the passenger door of her dad's car and got in. After more apologies and more assurances from her father that it was actually *his* fault that the woman had run into them, he got back in and started up the engine again.

The drawbridge was let down and they drove over the moat and up to the school. Cassie looked down into the moat as they crossed over. It looked very clean, with neatly trimmed fish gliding gracefully through the water. As they got closer to the castle, she could see that the ivy wasn't crawling freely over the walls at all, it was brutally clipped and only went exactly where it was meant to go. There was a carved stone fountain in the middle of the entrance forecourt with thin spouts of water like smug synchronised swimmers, all diving in perfect arcs with smiles on their faces. And straight lines of cars were radiating out from the fountain like beams out of the sun in a child's drawing. In fact, everything she saw made her feel like yelling and waving her arms about madly, just to mess up the perfect neatness of it all. Parents were unloading cases from their boots and passing them to uniformed porters who took them in through the grand main entrance, their feet crunching briskly over the gravel. There was a hum of excitement as older girls chatted eagerly, and spurts of laughter as they examined each other's new haircuts and clothes.

Cassie wished she could stay in the car forever and never get out, just sit in this same position with her dad next to her and the windows closed, safe. She couldn't bear to say goodbye either; it would be like admitting that she was staying. So she just kissed her father on the cheek quickly, opened the car door, and ran off to join the group of girls that was gathering around a woman who held a placard saying 'Year 7'. The new Year 7s were all smiling at each other nervously and staying close to the tall, bony woman, who squeezed their shoulders hard and ticked them off on her list.

'Cassie March,' announced Cassie crossly, going straight up to her. She was desperate to get into her dormitory away from these crowds of happy girls.

'Ah, Cassandra! "Cassie," is it? Is your father with you? There's tea for the parents in the hall.'

'He's parking, I think.'

'Well, you're in Fonteyn. Named after Margot Fonteyn, the dancer,' she beamed down at Cassie from a great height. Then suddenly she turned and called out over the crowds of heads, 'Bella!'

A freckly-faced girl, with brown hair in pig-tails and hundreds of small hairclips dotted all over her head, bounced over to them.

'Yes, Miss Chivers?'

Miss Chivers bent down to Cassie, 'Bella's in Year 8 dear and she's in Fonteyn too. Take Cassie up to the dorm will you, Bella.'

'Sure,' she smiled warmly.

'And Bella, those hairclips don't look regulation school colours to me, so I trust I won't see them in your hair after today.'

7

'No, Miss Chivers, of course not. Just enjoying my last moments of freedom.'

Bella turned to Cassie and grinned at her as if they had just hatched a mischievous plan.

'Come on, follow me,' she said as she marched off.

'Are we all dancers in Fonteyn?' asked Cassie, as they climbed up the final twisting wooden stairway.

'Me? A dancer? No way – look at me! No, I'm an actress.' She curtsied and then took a bow. 'We're mixed up in the dorms – dancers, singers and actors,' Bella went on to explain. 'Two Year 7s and two Year 8s in each dorm.'

The door was made of dark wooden boards held together by huge iron hinges. Bella lifted the latch, pushed hard and the door squealed open.

'Here we are,' she announced. 'Don't worry, you'll soon get used to all the old creaks and squeaks.'

Fonteyn was on the top floor so that from the window you could see the coast in the distance. Bella introduced Cassie to their other roommates – Jasmine, a Year 7 dancer, and Megan, a Year 8 singer – who were already unpacking. Jasmine had very pale skin and long flame-red hair. She smiled nervously, then blushed and looked away when Cassie said hello.

Cassie went over to the windows to look out and her heart skipped when she saw the shimmering sea down at Castletop Cove in the distance. She felt like leaping from the window in a massive dive straight into the cold choppy water. Starlight Academy was on a hill between Castletop Cove and Briar Bay, and Cassie resolved then and there that as soon as she got the chance, she would slip away down to the sea. It didn't look far, but she reckoned that once you had got through the forest and down the hill and then over the dunes, it would probably take about an hour. She would go at the weekend on her own. She didn't want to wait for some organized school outing. It was still September and not all that cold – there must be one last swim left in the summer. There was nothing quite like scrambling over crumbling rocks and running straight into the salty-stinging waves.

'Wakey-wakey!' Bella sang in her ear, and she jumped. Bella laughed, 'I'm glad to see you two are nice quiet Year 7s who know your place. Some of them flounce in all full of themselves on day one. But I think we'll all get along just fine.'

Cassie's cases soon arrived and she began unpacking so that she could be busy doing something and wouldn't have to talk to anyone. Bella and Megan kept up a constant stream of conversation about who they'd seen and what they'd done over the summer holidays.

'Tara's just as bad as ever,' Megan began. 'You know Daisy's pool party –'

'Oh I was *so* annoyed I missed that – especially as we were just in the boring old Lake District walking up hills in the rain,' said Bella. 'I'm constantly amazed by what my parents think makes a great holiday.'

'Well anyway,' continued Megan, 'Tara turned up in a skimpy designer bikini of course – probably hoping that

Daisy's brothers would all be there but they were away on some camp ha ha – and she insisted on showing us all her tan lines from the Bahamas. And she didn't even go in the pool –'

'– in case it ruined her hair.'

'Exactly. Poor Daisy's in Hepburn with her this year. Oh, and there were hot-dogs and pizza and ice-cream and she just nibbled on crackers and a box of salad that she had brought with her!'

Cassie couldn't help listening to their endless tales of summer escapades and envying their closeness. She couldn't imagine ever feeling as comfortable and normal as they seemed to. Her life so far had been quite solitary and she had liked it that way. Her only friend from primary school was Milo, the boy who lived next door, and they often went off to Highgate woods together at the weekend and made camps, but a lot of the time she just wandered about on her own. Cassie lifted her mother's ballet shoes out of her case and wondered where to put them. It was strange, she had never met her mother – at least not in her memory – and yet through the shoes, she felt as if she knew her. In fact, to her, her mother *was* this pair of ballet shoes. They had character: they were beautiful but scuffed and somehow, with their tattered ribbons, carefree and fun-loving, just as she imaged her mum had been. It wasn't something that made her sad, it was just her way of knowing her mum. In the end, she decided to slip the shoes under her bed because she needed them close by, but not exactly on show.

Next she took out the new laptop her dad had bought her as a goodbye present. It was sleek and black and she loved it, and the first chance she got she was going to email Milo and get his help on how to escape. She and Milo had grown up together like brother and sister, except that they didn't fight, and his life was carrying on as normal at the local secondary school. He had always stood up for her at primary school if anyone teased her for being boyish or for being such a good dancer, and she wondered what she would do without him. The night before she left to come to Starlight Academy, they had built a bonfire out in Milo's garden and sat around it toasting marshmallows and making up bad jokes. That was a game they played – making up the worst possible joke. She remembered his one from that night, which she had beaten.

'What's a vampire's favourite fruit?'

'Blood orange.'

'No, neck-tarine.'

'Oh wait, I've got an even worse one than that. What does a vampire eat for breakfast?'

'Blood orange?'

'No, Ready-neck. You know, like ready brek.'

'No way,' he had protested, 'that doesn't work at all! That's rubbish.'

'It's *meant* to be rubbish, you idiot.'

Now she was beginning to wonder if she would ever get a moment of peace or privacy to email him. When did you ever get to be on your own in a place like this?

Cassie layered her leotards carefully in the deep drawer of her bedside chest and hung up her tutu in the shared wardrobe. Then she stuffed the rest of her clothes into the remaining drawers and last of all hung her crisp new uniform in the wardrobe. There was a grey pleated skirt and a red gingham shirt, with a red tie and a red and grey v-necked jumper. She would have to get used to red and grey. Cassie had never worn a uniform before, and secretly she was quite pleased with it, although she had protested to her dad that it would be just like being in prison. As she listened to the bubbly chatter of the other two, she felt more and more lonely and found that she was suddenly longing to see the girl who had been sitting in the back of the car which had crashed into theirs. In this sea of strange faces, she felt somehow like a familiar old friend, even though Cassie had only met her moments before the others, and then had not really *met* her so much as frowned at her. She realised she didn't even know her name.

Cassie had just finished unpacking when a bell rang and Bella shouted, 'Dinner time! Drop everything! Most important part of the day. Must keep our strength up for all the gossiping that still lies ahead. Come on you two.'

As they were walking towards the dining hall, Cassie saw the girl from the back seat of the car and waved at her. The girl waved and smiled back, and then made her way over. She had changed her clothes and was now dressed in a silky silver halter-neck dress with a pink feather boa and gold strappy sandals, whereas everyone else, Cassie included, was still in their jeans and T-shirts.

'Shall we sit together?' the girl said. 'It's so awful walking in on your own and having no one to go to, isn't it? It's like walking into the wrong party. What's your name?'

'Cassie. What's yours?'

'Flo. But all the teachers here seem to be calling me Florence, which I think I prefer. Sounds far more sophisticated. What are you?'

'Dancer,' replied Cassie, 'you?'

'Singer. Thank goodness I can sing. It was my ticket out of the den of boys.'

They found two spare places and as soon as they had sat down, they found their plates piled high with sausages, mashed potato and peas, with glugs of thick gravy poured from above.

'Proper meals!' drooled Flo with delight. 'At home we have to eat whatever we can find lying around.'

'You dressed up,' said Cassie, waving her fork at Flo's outfit.

'I know. A Year 8 girl in my dorm told me everyone dresses up for dinner. She's called Tara. She's a dancer and she's really pretty.' Flo looked around the room and wrinkled up her nose. 'Doesn't look like we *are* supposed to dress up for dinner though, does it?'

'No,' said Cassie. 'How mean of her – and on your first day too.'

'Oh, I don't mind,' said Flo cheerfully. 'I quite like

dressing up. And I'm determined to be more girly anyway.'

'Why?' said Cassie, feeling slightly irritated with her silky ball-gown.

'Oh, you know, I've got all these brothers and I was the youngest, so when I came along, Mum just carried on as if I was a boy too. I've only just recently persuaded her to buy me a dress.'

'I see what you mean.'

'What do you think?' she looked down at her outfit. 'I bought most of it in a charity shop before I came. But the feather boa is my best bit – isn't it great? It's just so completely un-boyish. It was a present from my aunt. She's really glamorous, nothing like my mum. Isn't it great?' she repeated.

'Yeah, it's great,' said Cassie, a bit half-heartedly. Then added, 'It definitely is un-boyish,' because she felt she needed to say something else.

Despite her outfit, Cassie was beginning to like Flo more and more. She was so cheerful about everything that you couldn't help feeling happy yourself. And it *was* nice to have someone to sit with. But that didn't mean she was staying, she reminded herself. Before long, their plates were taken away and the headmistress Mrs Frost, sitting in the middle of the teachers' table at the top of the room, stood up and tinkled a small brass bell. There was immediate silence and all the girls looked her way expectantly. She smiled around at them all and then spoke in a sharp, clear voice, 'Well, it's wonderful to see so many new faces, and equally wonderful to see all the old faces – *most* of them, that is.' She smiled knowingly and there was a short burst of laughter from the older girls. 'Welcome, girls. I'm sure you will love it here at Starlight Academy. You are all talented artists in your field – that is why you are here, and you should be proud of that. And we hope that during your years at the Academy you will learn to respect the importance of discipline too. No performer, however talented, ever achieves her true potential without discipline.'

She smiled again, as if to reassure them briefly that she wasn't too serious, and then clapped once.

'And on that note, let's enjoy some pudding. As soon as you have finished, you may leave the table and return to your dorms to finish unpacking. Any dawdlers can help with the clearing up. Lights out half an hour earlier tonight at eight thirty. You've all had a very eventful day and we want you fresh for your first lessons tomorrow morning. Good night and sleep well.'

As soon as she finished speaking, pudding trolleys came clattering down the rows and steaming slabs of apple pie and ice-cream were handed out.

'I just *love* all these rules, don't you?' whispered Flo eagerly. 'I love the bells. I love the way meals always happen at the same time and you have to eat then or never. And I love lights out and … and … that you have to make your bed in the morning. Don't you?'

Cassie was giving her a weird look and Flo suddenly looked embarrassed.

'Oh sorry, you don't know what my house is like. A complete mess. My mum rescues chickens. And there are no rules. And my mum never really notices if I'm there or not.'

'Neither does my dad,' said Cassie, 'but in a good way. I like it like that. He lets me be free.'

Cassie thought about how she and her dad could sit in the same room, reading or fiddling or making something, and not talk for hours, but in a warm friendly way, just being with each other. She thought of their meals of toast and jam at midnight and their endless pyjama days. The thought of him at home on his own, perhaps trying to cook dinner for himself, brought a lump to her throat.

'I can't *stand* all these rules,' she said passionately. 'They're so unnecessary. As if it really matters what time the lights go out – it's ridiculous!'

'Oh I love lights out! It's so definite. And it's always so noisy in my house, you never get a word in and there's always someone having a crisis more important than yours. I know there are even more of us here, but I still feel more important than I do at home. Matron has already asked me what my favourite breakfast cereal is and my mum has *never* asked me that in all the eleven years I've lived with her.'

'I can't *stand* all this interfering in your life all the time,' said Cassie crossly, 'wanting to know what your favourite cereal is – it's none of their business! Aren't we allowed to keep anything to ourselves? They'll be asking us what colour knickers we're wearing next. I just want to be left alone!'

Cassie slammed her spoon down on the table to make her point.

'Oh.' Flo's face fell in disappointment. She chewed her lip and looked around the room. Cassie realised immediately that she had said the wrong thing, but she didn't know what to say to put it right.

'I didn't mean you. I didn't mean I want *you* to leave me alone.'

Flo shrugged.

'It doesn't matter.'

She finished off her pudding quickly without saying anything. When she had finished, she put her spoon down, looked around again as if she was supposed to be meeting someone, then got up and walked out of the dining hall.

Cassie left the hall too and headed straight for the back door. She had noticed it on the way to the dining hall. It was tucked away at the end of a dark corridor by the kitchens and it led out to the playing fields. She just *had* to get out of this building. What if she didn't *want* to go straight from the dining hall to her bedroom and finish unpacking and go straight to bed? Wasn't there any room for variation? Were they all just robots who would do exactly the same thing at exactly the same time every day, day in day out, from now until eternity? She stormed along the gloomy corridor, getting hotter and crosser with every step, but just as she was about to reach the back door, Miss Chivers, the tall thin teacher who had registered them when they arrived, caught sight of her.

'Are you lost, dear?' she said putting her long arm round Cassie's shoulder and giving it a tight squeeze.

'No, I just thought I'd go for a quick wander about before bed,' said Cassie, feeling irritated that she couldn't walk five steps without bumping into someone.

Miss Chivers laughed nervously, as if she wasn't sure whether Cassie was joking or not.

'I suppose you might not know all the rules yet,' she said, 'but no one in Year 7 is allowed outside after seven pm.'

Cassie raised her eyes and huffed, 'It's OK, I'll come back. It's not like I'm going to go and *live* out there or anything.'

The smile dropped off Miss Chivers' face in an instant, like jelly sliding off a spoon.

'Perhaps I should warn you, Cassandra March, that contrary to the way you may have been accustomed to living, at Starlight Academy you will *not* just do as you please. Now go up to your dormitory immediately and in future do not address a teacher in that tone.'

Cassie was so shocked at Miss Chivers' sudden transformation from Red Riding-Hood's Granny to terrifying wolf that she dashed upstairs without another word.

Cassie lay in bed that night feeling utterly miserable. Not only was this school insufferably strict, but she had already managed to ruin her one chance of friendship. Why couldn't she just keep her mouth shut? When would she learn not to just say whatever was in her head? Just before bed, she had managed to send Milo a quick text:

greetings from prison cant wait til they release me at half-term hows it going at your school? But his reply had only made her more miserable: *great loads of new friends* and that was all. The lights were finally out and Bella and Megan had finally finished chatting in whispers, when Cassie heard a muffled sob from the bed next to hers.

'Are you OK?' she whispered across the space between hers and Jasmine's beds.

'I want to go home,' Jasmine whispered between her stifled sobs.

'So do I,' said Cassie. She stretched her arm across to Jasmine's bed and held her hand in the darkness.

Chapter 2: *Making Friends (and enemies)*

Cassie lay awake for some time, planning how to escape. She could fake a serious illness, but she'd never been very good at that; or get herself expelled – but her dad would be so upset – or maybe she could say *he* had a life-threatening illness and needed her home, but that might be bad luck, and what if he really got one? She lay there in the darkness, her head buzzing with ideas, and thought the whole night would pass in that way, but suddenly she found that she was being awoken by a clanging bell and it was morning. The room around her began to shuffle awake. Bella groaned from across the room, 'Urgh! The first morning is always the worst. That bell! It makes me dream about fire-engines all night long.'

Megan agreed, 'After a long lazy summer, it just seems so cruel. I haven't got up before nine for weeks.'

'You're lucky,' said Bella, 'my parents think the day's wasted if you don't get up with the birds. Never let me sleep in. There's always some museum or art gallery that requires our immediate presence.'

And they were off, talking and laughing together as if they had never stopped for the night. Everyone else in the room had laid their uniforms out over their bedside chairs the night before, but Cassie had refused, determined not to follow what everyone else did. So she was still scrabbling about in her drawers and wardrobe when everyone else was ready to go down to breakfast, and they all had to wait for her.

In the dining hall, Cassie caught sight of Flo and waved at her hopefully, wondering if she would still be feeling hurt by her stupid comments of the night before. But to her surprise, Flo waved back just as enthusiastically as ever and came over to sit with her.

'I'm so excited,' she began before they had even sat down, 'it's my week for choosing the cereal. Did you know they do that here? I think it's a brilliant idea. Every Year 7 girl gets to choose a cereal for the week. I've chosen muesli because all we get at home is sugary cardboard rubbish that my brothers buy.'

'I'm sorry I was such a grump yesterday,' said Cassie.

'Were you? Oh, sorry, I didn't notice. There's Tara.' She waved across at a beautiful tall girl on another table, who completely ignored her. The tall girl had a long black scarf wrapped around her neck.

'Did I tell you? She's in my dorm. She's in Year 8,' explained Flo breathlessly. 'She's got a sore throat. She can hardly speak, poor thing. But she's a dancer so it won't affect her performance at least.'

Cassie was beginning to dislike Tara already.

'Yes, she looks like the kind of girl who would always have something wrong with her,' she said.

'What do you mean?' asked Flo.

'You know, never happy unless everyone's feeling sorry for her.'

'Oh, I don't think she *is* like that,' said Flo, looking puzzled. 'She's just got a sore throat, that's all.'

Cassie wished again that she hadn't said anything. It seemed like every time she opened her mouth she ended up sounding like a witch.

'What's the first lesson?' she asked, to change the subject.

'Maths, would you believe it? Talk about throwing us in at the deep end. I can't wait for the first singing class this afternoon though.'

'We've got ballet first this afternoon. Ballet every day, plus jazz on Tuesdays and tap on Thursdays,' said Cassie, consulting her folded up timetable. She had decided to carry it around in her pocket so that she had some hope of being in the right place at the right time.

They had cleared away their breakfast things onto the trolley in the corner and were just about to leave the dining hall, when Tara finally responded to Flo's wave and came over to them.

'Hi Tara,' smiled Flo, 'this is my friend Cassie. She's a dancer too.'

Tara looked Cassie up and down and slowly raised her eyebrows, 'Really? Sorry, I would have guessed you were an actress. You know, useful for the boy parts and all that.'

Cassie was so taken aback that she didn't know what to say.

'I know,' laughed Flo, as if Tara hadn't said anything bad, 'she does look kind of boyish, but she's really pretty too, don't you think?'

Tara shrugged sceptically.

* * *

Mr Broccoli the Maths teacher rang a bell on his desk and after a few moments there was silence in the room. He had let them have three minutes to laugh at his name and was now calling a halt to it. Although generally it was difficult to laugh when someone gave you permission to, there had been a few initial hoots, which had gradually erupted into proper giggles and soon the whole room was shaking with laughter.

'Good,' he said. 'That's got that over and done with. It's an Italian name by the way. Please open your text books to Chapter Three on Algebra.'

Cassie loved Maths, and she loved Algebra most of all, although she didn't admit it, and groaned along with everyone else when it was mentioned. She particularly loved the beautiful steps of equations, the way you re-arranged everything into the best possible order, then gradually stripped it down to its bare bones, and came at last to the clear answer. It was like a perfect dance in your head. Mr Broccoli wrote an equation up on the board:

Find a:
$$4a \times 5a = 60$$

He scanned the room and then looked down at the list of names on his desk, 'Jasmine.'

Jasmine turned bright red and looked like she was trying to smell the text-book on her desk.

'Start us off. What do we do first?'

'Splimpify,' Jasmine stumbled in a shaky voice. There were a few sniggers and Cassie glared around the room at the sniggerers. 'I mean simplify,' she said to the desk in a muffled voice, desperate for her turn to be over.

'That's right. We do the multiplication of the 'a's.'

Mr Broccoli squeaked some numbers on the board. Cassie had already worked out the answer to this problem, and the next, and was moving on to the third in her head when Mr Broccoli said, 'And Cassandra, what happens to the 20 when we take it over to the other side?'

She looked up at him blankly, caught off guard, 'Um …' her eyes darted back to the question in the book, but she had lost track of where they were.

'Thought so. No time for daydreaming in Maths, Cassandra.'

'I wasn't daydreaming. And my name's Cassie.'

He fixed her with a hard stare.

'You can call it what you like, Cassandra. Daydreaming, thinking, pondering a solution to world peace, it doesn't matter. No time off in Maths. Now, Abigail –'

'Wait,' Cassie protested, 'I know the answer now.'

'Hands up, please. Abigail, can you tell us what happens to the 20 when we take it to the other side?'

Cassie put her hand up and waited, but Abigail answered and the lesson moved on.

Cassie's face went hot with indignation and her feet began to itch, which always happened when she was angry. It made her want to stamp hard on the floor, but she settled for kicking herself in the ankle as quietly as she could. She didn't want to get in trouble on the first day.

At break, they all went out into the sunlight with their fruit buns and a group of Year 7s sat on the sloping lawn which led down to the lake. Cassie began picking the raisins out of her bun and flicking them into the air.

'What are you doing?' asked Flo, mystified.

'Getting rid of the raisins of course,' said Cassie.

'How can you not like raisins?' Flo asked. 'They're yummy.'

'Not if you don't like them they're not. Anyway, I'm allergic to them.'

'Really?'

'Well, no, not strictly. I just hate the way they pretend to be sweets when really they're just dead grapes.'

'I think I might be allergic to algebra: it makes my head hurt,' groaned Flo. 'That reminds me, Tara was telling me that she's allergic to the material of the school uniform.'

'She would be,' said Cassie.

'She has to have special uniforms made in a different material, and she secretly gets them to alter the design, which must be why she looks so good in it. Anyway, you've got her all wrong, Cassie. She's really friendly. Seriously, she is. You'd realise if you got to know her properly.'

'Well, I guess I will soon. We'll be in the same ballet class this afternoon.'

A frisbee came flying past them and Flo jumped up to get it, but as she darted off down the slope she tripped over her feet and tumbled head over heels, landing at the bottom with her legs in the air. There was laughter all around, except from Jasmine who wailed, 'Stop laughing at her! Don't be so mean!'

But even Flo was smiling as she walked back up the slope to join them, her grassy hair sticking up all over the place.

'It's no use,' she puffed. 'I'll never be elegant and sophisticated.'

She sat down and tried to rearrange her wayward hair.

'Oh no, my hair-band has snapped,' she groaned. 'I can't go into lessons like this.'

'Here, borrow this,' said Cassie, taking a band off her wrist.

'Thanks, but I can't wear that,' said Flo anxiously, 'it's not school colours.'

'Don't worry, I'm sure it won't contaminate you,' said Cassie, returning the band to her wrist.

It had come out sounding nastier than she had meant to, and in the awkward silence she felt everyone looking at her.

To avoid their eyes, Cassie lay back on the grass and stared up at the cloudless sky.

'It's such a beautiful day. It seems so wrong to be stuck inside looking at books. I think I'll go for a wander.'

Flo looked at her watch, 'You can't, you haven't got time. We have to be back in five minutes.'

'You really do like your rules, don't you?' said Cassie. 'It's like you'd just dissolve if someone wasn't telling you what to do and where to go.'

For the first time, Flo looked hurt and Jasmine surprised everyone by speaking up, 'There's no need to be so rude to her. She's just trying to make sure you don't get in trouble.'

A few others said 'Yeah, exactly!' and Cassie felt like burying herself in the ground.

*   *   *

When she walked into her first ballet class that afternoon, Cassie was surprised to see an old lady sitting on a high stool in the corner of the room. Her dance teacher at home had been young and beautiful. This woman had grey hair and was wrinkled. Surely this couldn't be their teacher? She looked like a fortune-teller.

'Come in, come in,' she wobbled in a foreign accent, signalling with her arm towards the *barre* along which they should arrange themselves. There was a frown on her face and she seemed weary as she looked along the line of girls, nodding as if she had seen them all before and they were all just as she had expected.

'So, a new group of girls joins us. And some of you will be good and some poor and some so-so. My name, girls, is Princess Octavia Markova. I have been teaching Starlight Academy since very first day it was started by my dear friend Lady Anthea Price. You will learn much from me. I was once brilliant ballerina with Kirov ballet in Leningrad. Am still brilliant, but now,' she tapped her knees with her gnarled fingers, 'creaky bones. Now, stand at the *barre* and adopt first position.'

The girls all did as they were told, the new girls twitching with their eagerness to impress in the first lesson.

Princess Octavia walked up and down the line and then pointed at Tara, the Year 8 girl who was in Flo's dorm, 'You. What is your name? I forget.'

Tara looked slightly hurt and confused as she answered.

'Tara Davenport, Miss.'

'You will call me Princess Octavia. Or simply Princess. Certainly not Miss. I am not a kitchen maid. You are one who has natural poise and grace,' Tara's face lit up with pride as she waited to be pointed out as the example to follow. But Princess Octavia continued, 'Unfortunately in your girlhood you have been allowed to develop bad habits. Your leg is not properly turned out as it should be from the hip. Such an easy mistake.' She shook her head sadly, and then barked, 'Pull up. Lift those muscles. Turn outwards.'

Tara looked away angrily as she adjusted her leg, avoiding everyone's eyes. But Princess Octavia continued as if she had not said anything hurtful at all.

'You observe that some girls do not like to be corrected, because they think that they are already correct. And their teachers are too fond of them to correct them. Their teachers like them too much and do not want to make them unhappy. Not so me.'

She moved on down the line and corrected another girl's foot and another's shoulders. When she got to Cassie, she smiled for the first time.

'You have been well taught. I am not smiling at you. You must not think it is you who pleases me, but your teacher. You have been well taught and that is always pleasing to see.'

She clapped her hands sharply three times right next to Cassie's ear and Cassie jumped.

'Look at this girl here. She has near-perfect position. Her knees are turned out just right, her back is upright but maintains its natural curve, her head held strong and straight. But that does not mean,' she pinched Cassie's nose, 'that she will always have perfect position. She could lose it tomorrow if she does not practise and practise to be correct. And it is shame she looks like a ragamuffin street boy.'

Cassie tried not to look in Tara's direction but she could feel her eyes burning into her with hatred.

During the first lesson, and indeed throughout the whole term, Princess Octavia never made any effort to learn, or even to find out, any of their names, but referred to them in her own way as 'the one who has been well-taught', 'the one who sticks her elbows out', 'the one who thinks I am unkind', which could in fact have referred to any of them. Even Cassie, whom she often pointed out as the example of good position, didn't think her kind, though she couldn't help feeling secretly proud of herself.

'She says I've been well taught,' she told her dad on the phone one night, smiling with pleasure as she said it.

'That's good to hear – it's cost enough!' he replied.

'But Dad,' she couldn't help complaining, 'it's so strict here. You wouldn't believe what they have rules about. Like the other evening I went into tea with bare feet because it wasn't that cold and, well, you know, I've always gone around in bare feet. And they sent me straight back upstairs to put shoes on. And by the look on Mrs Frost's face, you'd have thought I was completely naked.'

Mr March laughed, 'Oh dear, they're going to think you've been brought up in the jungle by gorillas.'

Chapter 3: *In Trouble Already*

By the end of her second week at school, Cassie was feeling like a chicken in an over-crowded cage. There was plenty of space at the school, of course, and beautiful grounds, but you could never enjoy them, not unless you were being marched somewhere by a teacher to do some specific activity. There was no time to wander and explore, the whole day was divided up into lessons of one sort or another, and even after the end of the school day, there was always somewhere you had to be by a certain time. One night, she had decided to go outside and do some star-gazing. Milo had sent her a text at about seven o'clock saying there would be a really cool comet flying over that night and that she would have a good chance of seeing it out in the countryside. So she had slipped on her trainers and hoodie to go outside and take a look. But yet again, Miss Chivers, who seemed to patrol the doorways like a troll guard, caught her and she never got to see anything.

'I'm thinking of starting up a petition against the seven o'clock curfew' she told Flo after lunch the next day, as they were sitting outside under a tree.

'Oh, please don't,' said Flo, frowning against the sunlight, 'you'll just get in trouble and what's the point?'

'Get in trouble? For exercising my democratic rights? Maybe you're right. Maybe I should just go ahead and commit some kind of proper crime – I mean, I bet real criminals in prison get more freedom than us.'

'Well, I love it here!' beamed Flo. 'For once in my life I know exactly what I'm meant to be doing at every minute of the day. I feel like a soldier on parade, everything is so brilliantly worked out. Anyway, I don't know how you have time to get annoyed, there's so much to do.'

'I know there is, but it's all so organised and rigid. There's no spontaneity.'

'Oh stop complaining, Cassie,' said Flo, getting to her feet, 'it makes you look ugly.'

But Cassie was feeling desperate to break out. All she could think about was the sea – the shouting, crashing freedom of the waves, the swish and suck of water pulling back through the pebbles, the fresh salty smell of seaweed. She knew they wouldn't be able to get as far as the sea in one break time, but she wanted to at least begin to forge a path down there, make the first tracks.

'Come on,' she said, holding out a hand to Flo and pulling her up from the ground. 'Let's go exploring.'

'We can't!' said Flo, looking at her watch. 'Stop going on about it.'

Cassie took hold of Flo's wrist and looked at her watch.

'Look, we've got half an hour until the first lesson of the afternoon. Let's head for the woods. Come on!'

She began running and to her surprise looked back to see that Flo was following her, running too. Flo shrugged, 'I suppose it can't hurt. We're not breaking any rules after all.'

There was a small woodland at the edge of the school grounds and they were soon in the middle of it. The air was bright and fresh and the birds were all singing. Cassie and Flo stopped running and sat on a fallen tree-trunk, laughing happily.

'It was listening to a bird singing that first made me want to play the flute,' said Flo.

'Aw, how sweet,' said Cassie.

Flo shot her a suspicious sideways look.

'No, I *mean* it! I think it really *is* sweet. I can just see you as a little girl listening to a bird and trying to copy it. It's not fair! Now you think that everything I say is meant nastily.'

Flo beamed at her, 'No I don't. I was just checking – because, well, you said I should stop thinking everyone is nice all the time when they're not.'

The tree in front of them had a large hole at the top of its trunk.

'Let's climb up,' said Cassie. 'You never know what might be hidden in that hole. It's the perfect hiding place. Just think, there could be stolen jewels, secret love let-ters, anything.'

'No way. Forget it! I've come on an adventure with you, but I'm not going to start climbing trees. You know me, I'd tear my uniform straight away and then probably fall and break my arm.'

'OK, you stay here. I'm going up.'

Cassie easily scaled the lower branches, gliding like a cat up the trunk, but as she got higher, it got trickier. Suddenly there was a loud crack as a branch that she was standing on snapped off. Cassie yelped as her right foot swooped down. Luckily, she was holding on to a branch above and her left foot was secure, but for some time she hung there, her right leg swinging in the air, unable to put it anywhere.

'I think I'm stuck,' she squeaked, feeling genuinely frightened.

Flo couldn't help looking at her watch.

'Oh Cassie! You idiot!'

'Thanks.'

'But you love climbing trees,' Flo wailed, 'it's your thing. You *must* be able to find a way down.'

'I know, I know. But seriously I can't find anywhere to put my foot. I'm actually quite scared Flo.'

'Sorry.' Flo bit her lip and stood back to get a good look at the tree, but it didn't help much.

'OK, try putting that foot where your other foot is.'

'Can't, no room. That foot's slipping anyway,' said Cassie through pinched lips.

'OK, look, there's a branch much further down, but you'll have to let go of that branch you're holding onto and reach out for the one on your left so you can swing down.'

'I *really* don't want to.'

'You have to. It's the only way you'll get down.'

'Oh …' Cassie wailed, 'I'm not sure if I can reach.'

'Well if you're scared,' said Flo, 'then I'm *really* scared, so stop it right now.'

'OK, I'll try,' said Cassie, her voice trembling.

With one foot still on the tree and one hand clinging to a branch, Cassie stretched the other arm down and tried to grab hold of the lower branch. But she missed and swung outwards, the weight of her body almost prising her off the tree. Her body was now standing out sideways from the tree, like a flag shaking in the breeze. She started to whimper.

'Oh, Flo! I can't get it.'

'You *have* to. Push with that foot against the tree and swing your arm back round. Come on Cassie, you *have* to do it.'

It took some time, but slowly, in small careful movements, Flo managed to guide Cassie back down the tree. They had no idea how long it had taken, but by the time Cassie was safely on the ground, they realised that afternoon lessons would have started long ago. Cassie had a tap class with Mr Rossi – so at least it wouldn't be Princess Octavia she had to face – but Flo, even worse, had a private singing lesson.

'I'm *really* sorry,' said Cassie as they jogged back towards school, 'that was so dumb of me.'

Flo's face had gone white and for a while she didn't speak as they half-walked, half-ran through the woods. Then she just said quietly, 'I hate being late.'

'I know. I know you do. And I'm sorry, I really am.'

When they reached the front entrance of the school, they realised that their hope of somehow sneaking in unnoticed was ridiculous. Mrs Glasswell, Flo's singing teacher, was out the front making a call on her mobile, which she cancelled when she saw them walking up.

'We're so sorry Mrs Glasswell, it was all my fault,' said Cassie in what she hoped was a humble voice.

'Yes, I expect it was. I'll let Mr Rossi know you are safe and then you had better both come with me to the Head.'

Mrs Glasswell set off at a brisk pace and they followed close behind, skipping to keep up with her.

*   *   *

The Headmistress' office was exceptionally quiet and smelt of old books. Cassie and Flo stood nervously in front of Mrs Frost's desk while she finished writing something with a scratchy pen. Finally, she looked up.

'Well, girls, you've already heard my speech on the first night about the importance of discipline, so you already know how disappointed I am about this slack behaviour. It shows a complete disregard for your teachers and, quite frankly, for yourselves.'

'It wasn't disregard,' Cassie argued, 'I got stuck up a tree.'

'Cassandra!' Mrs Frost barked. 'Do not speak unless I ask you to.'

Cassie literally gulped in fright. She had never felt frightened of anyone before. Why should this lady frighten her? It annoyed her. Mrs Frost was beautiful in a stern kind of way, her dark brown hair was cut in a neat bob which lightly brushed her sharp cheekbones.

Her clothes were immaculate and a string of perfectly round pearls sat obediently on her elegant neck. As she felt her heart fluttering in her chest, Cassie realised with horror that she wanted to please Mrs Frost. It was not a familiar feeling – she had never really minded before what people thought of her – but it was certainly true, she desperately wanted Mrs Frost to like her.

'Now, I don't mind if you were up a tree in the school grounds or up a mountain in Peru, you should have made sure you were back in time for the start of your lesson. Is that understood?'

'But I –'

Mrs Frost slapped her desk with a slicing sound like a head being chopped clean off.

'Enough! I said is that understood?'

'Yes, Mrs Frost,' they both chimed. There was something about the way she spoke which had almost made Cassie say 'Yes, your highness' but luckily she didn't as it would definitely have been taken as rudeness.

'At this school, you will follow the rules to the letter. The primary purpose of our founder Lady Price in setting up Starlight Academy was to give artistic performers a basic training in self-discipline. As a punishment for being late, you will be grounded within school buildings for two weeks. You may only go outside for timetabled sports lessons, when obviously you will be accompanied by a teacher. Otherwise, during any break or leisure periods, you will remain within school buildings in the company of your housemistress.'

Cassie and Flo could say nothing to excuse themselves and they left Mrs Frost's office as quickly as possible.

Their housemistress Miss Mackenzie was a squashy, grey-haired woman who smelt of talcum-powder; she was sweet and gentle but she kept to the rules rigidly. Since they were in trouble, she tried not to talk to Cassie and Flo too much, in case she found herself being too kind, but she stuck to them like velcro. When she was on her rounds of the dorms during break they had to follow her in silence. After school, when they could hear all the other girls shrieking and throwing leaves at each other in the last few pink moments before sunset, they had to sit in her over-heated room on low, uncomfortable armchairs, reading. It felt to Cassie like being trapped in an old-people's home for an eternal afternoon.

On that first afternoon, as they sat in the quiet of her room with books open on their laps, staring longingly out of the window, Cassie whispered, 'I do think they were over-reacting a bit.'

Flo, who was looking more anxious than ever, didn't say anything, which made Cassie feel even more dreadful, so she carried on talking, 'I mean we didn't kill anyone. Or steal anything. It's not one of the Ten Commandments, you know, Thou Shalt Not Be Late.'

Flo sniggered at last and Cassie breathed a sigh of relief.

'Oh phew, you don't hate me then?'

'No, how could I? You can't help it. Anyway, I suppose it will do me some good to get in trouble for once.'

'Well, I'm going to make sure they understand it wasn't at all your fault.'

'Yes it was. I do have a mind of my own you know. I decided to come with you and I knew what you were like.'

At night time, just before lights out, Cassie sent furious emails to Milo:

```
It's stupidly strict here — you
wouldn't believe it. They're total-
ly against freedom and originality.
They want us all to be exactly the
same and do exactly what we're told
to do when they pull the strings,
like a line of identical puppets.
As you can imagine, it's pretty
difficult to have any fun.
```

Even as she wrote it, she knew it wasn't strictly true. Milo's replies anyway were disappointingly brief. Just: Sounds rubbish. And another time: Cheer up, nearly half-term. When she asked him what school was like at his end, he just said: Yeah, cool, loads of new friends and that was it. Often he didn't even reply at all and she began to get fed up of the sound of her own voice moaning on and on.

At last, the two weeks of torture were up and Cassie and Flo celebrated by spending the whole evening on the tennis courts, playing and chatting in the late afternoon sun. It was one of those beautiful autumn evenings full of the smell of bonfires and the crunch of red-gold leaves. The Half-term Sports Day was coming up: it included a school-wide tennis tournament and a house hockey match, and there were trials for the house team the next day. Cassie was terrible at hockey but pretty good at tennis and Flo was the opposite, so they helped each other to improve with tips and encouragement. After an hour of practising both, they flopped down exhausted on the tennis court, relishing the freedom of being outside. It was getting cold but they were still hot from playing and wanted to enjoy the red sunset to its very end before it dropped off the world.

'Well, thank God only *one* of my brothers can come to the Half-term tournament thingy,' said Flo as she pulled on her sweatshirt. 'I couldn't bear the thought of *all* the great ugly beasts lining up and booing me.'

Cassie shot her a quizzical look.

'What are you talking about? How come your *brother* is coming?'

'Well, families are invited to the Sports Day aren't they?'

'No, I don't think so,' said Cassie. 'First I've heard of it, anyway.'

'They are, I'm sure they are,' Flo protested. 'Tara told me.'

Cassie groaned, 'Oh Flo! You've got to stop listening to her.'

'Is she joking again?'

'Well, joking's a nice way of putting it' said Cassie. 'I bet I know why she did it – she's probably heard that you've got lots of brothers. You know how boy-mad she is. Come on,' she said, pulling Flo to her feet, 'we'd better go and call your parents to tell them it's off.'

Chapter 4: *Secret Party*

As it happened, Mrs Frost was in the school office when Flo went in for permission to call home, and when she heard what Flo had been told – about families being invited to the sports tournament – a smile spread across her face.

'What a splendid idea! We can make it a Family Fun Day, with games for all the family and a big tea in the hall,' she said. 'And then you can all go home a day early for Half-term. I wonder why I didn't think of it myself.' She turned to one of the school secretaries: 'We'll have to get a letter out tomorrow.'

Bella and Megan laughed their heads off in the dorm when Cassie told them what had happened.

'Tara will be gutted. She's always trying to make sure no one ever meets her parents.'

'Why, what's wrong with them?' asked Cassie.

'Well, her dad's really posh – a lord or something I think – but really quiet and meek. And her mum's the opposite, huge and loud, and she dresses as if she's sixteen. Tara's really embarrassed about them.'

The week before Half-term, Cassie got a package from her dad. She ran up to her dorm at lunch-break to open it and it was full of chocolate, and books, and music and other cool stuff, including a bandana and a pair of earrings, which he had brought back from a business trip to Mexico. He was a furniture-maker and had been there researching Aztec designs. The bandana was purple with green cactuses on it and the earrings were massive hoops with turquoise stones dangling off them, and she loved them both. With a sudden lump in her throat, Cassie rolled the bandana up and tied it in her hair. Then she hooked the earrings into her ears. She didn't care what the rules were, this was a present from her dad and she missed him.

'Uh-oh,' said Bella when she looked up and saw Cassie. Then she tutted in mock disapproval and wagged her finger. '*Definitely* not school colours, Cassandra.'

'I don't care,' Cassie huffed. 'God, sometimes I'm amazed they don't make us dye our hair red and paint our faces grey. It would suit this school – grey faces.'

'Cheer up!' laughed Bella. 'School's only for term-time, you know. There's the rest of life, as well. And weekends. It's not such a big deal.'

Before she had even reached the breakfast room, Cassie had the misfortune of bumping into Mrs Frost, who took one look at the bandana and the earrings and called her over. Cassie felt a sudden surge of panic; her earlier bravado seemed to have melted away entirely. Nevertheless, she tried to saunter over carelessly, whilst tugging nervously on her hoop earring. The sauntering was a mistake, it turned out. By the time she reached Mrs Frost's side, she could see the pulse of anger throbbing in her neck.

'Cassandra March,' she said, her voice like clippers beheading roses, 'a pupil at Starlight Academy wears Starlight Academy uniform and nothing else.'

'It's just that my dad –'

'It is just nothing. You will return to your room this minute and remove those items.'

Cassie stared in fury at Mrs Frost's perfect, glossy helmet of hair and felt a sudden urge to ruffle it. She scowled hard but kept her mouth firmly shut as the head-mistress walked off, clacking her heels briskly on the stone floor.

By now, all of Cassie's fear had turned to anger, an anger so loud and piercing that it made her ears ring. How *dare* Mrs Frost speak to her like that! How *dare* she call her precious presents 'those items'! How *dare* she refuse to even listen! She stormed upstairs, plotting revenge. Once inside the dorm, she stomped around slamming drawers and kicking doors, desperately searching for a way to get back at the school for trapping her so tightly in its corset of rules that she could hardly breathe. But on the way back down to breakfast, she ran into Bella who grabbed her arm and told her in hurried excitement, 'It's Daisy's birthday today and there's a secret party in Hepburn tonight.'

'Great!' said Cassie, cheering up instantly at the thought of doing something even remotely off-timetable. And then, suddenly embarrassed, she added, 'Oh, am I invited or are you just telling me about it?'

'Of course you're invited, you loon!' laughed Bella.

'It's only for Fonteyn and Hepburn girls though. We're going to dress up as ridiculously as possible. You know Daisy and her clothes – I think she wants us all to look as whacky as her.'

Daisy was the most eccentric girl in the entire school. Despite the strict rules, she somehow managed to be individual and unique. Underneath her curtain of smooth brown hair, the back of her head was secretly shaved, but she wore it in a low ponytail so you couldn't tell, and she had piercings all the way up both ears. Even though she wasn't allowed to wear any earrings in them, you could still see them. And at weekends, she really went to town, and wore a mish-mash of clothes that no-one else would think of putting together, like vintage tweed shorts from a charity shop teamed with pink neon leggings and army boots, and a flowery, frilly blouse. She was also immensely talented. She was the only girl in the school who did dance, drama *and* singing, and at the age of twelve she had already written a musical and choreographed it herself.

'I'm in charge of the music,' Bella continued, 'and the rest of you have to bring some food – nothing spectacular, just as much junk as you can possibly lay your hands on.'

*   *   *

It was seven o'clock, two hours before lights out, and the party was about to begin. All the girls in Fonteyn had dressed up in the weirdest clothes they could find and poured their joint stores of make-up and accessories into a bag.

'I've got a film camera thing,' said Megan, just as they were about to leave the dorm, 'at least I think that's what it is.' She gave it a baffled look. 'No idea how it works. My parents bought it for me. They want me to record school life for them so they can see what it's like, but I don't see the point when I can just tell them what it's like. Should I bring it?'

Megan's parents were on a constant mission to bring her into the twenty first century, but she couldn't work a computer, didn't want an iPod or a mobile, and preferred writing letters to emailing or texting. Her mum was a cutting-edge fashion designer and her dad an independent record-producer, but Megan was resolutely uncool. She had no interest in modern life and liked nothing more than reading a book, going for a walk, painting or sewing. Her mum had almost given up taking her shopping and buying her fantastic clothes, because she showed no interest and never wore them.

'Oh my God, it's not fair,' moaned Bella for the hundredth time. 'I wish you could lend me your mum for a week. We could go shopping, do lunch, she could take me to all the celebrity parties. *I* wouldn't disappoint her. And you could follow my parents around ancient churches and art galleries. Oh *please* let's swap!'

'Look, should I bring this thing or not?' repeated Megan.

'Of course! We can do a fashion show and film it. Come on, let's go.'

They all piled into Hepburn where Daisy, Tara, Flo and Freya were waiting. The Fonteyn girls added their own stash to the food table which was already overflowing with popcorn, crisps and neon chewy sweets. The room was filled with pink and black balloons and a space had been cleared in the middle of the floor for dancing.

'Drink?' said Daisy, and poured them all a plastic cup of Coke frothed up with a blob of melting ice-cream.

Everyone was dressed in the weirdest mixture of clothes they could find. Flo was wearing her pyjamas, her wellies, a wide-brimmed sunhat with pink sunglasses and her beloved pink feather boa. Daisy was wearing a leather jacket over what looked like a table-cloth, her school tie around her head and high wedge sandals. Tara and Freya were the only ones who hadn't followed the dress code. While the rest of them were wrapped in brightly coloured, mismatched items, Tara wore a tight white mini-dress and glossy red heels, and Freya was still in her school uniform.

'Tara!' shrieked Bella. 'There aren't any boys coming you know.'

But Tara just raised her eyebrows knowingly, 'You should always look your best, you never know *who* might turn up. At the very least,' she continued with a spiky look in Cassie's direction, 'you should wash your face and brush your hair. Sadly, some people don't even make that small effort.'

Cassie frowned in annoyance and rubbed her sleeve across her face in case it was grubby.

'Well, if you're expecting a celebrity appearance,' laughed Bella, 'I think Mrs Frost is the closest we're going to get – and let's hope *she* doesn't turn up.'

Then she plugged in her iPod and the cheesy dance music began to pump out of the speakers.

With foaming drinks in hand, the girls began to dance madly to the music, all except one girl: Freya. Freya, the other Year 7 girl in Hepburn, who was a singer like Flo, was sulking on a chair in the corner. She looked like she would rather be anywhere else and had absolutely no intention of entering into the spirit of the party. Cassie looked over in her direction. Freya was in her class but she realised that she had never spoken to her, mainly because she looked so scary. She had long dark scraggy hair and a permanent frown and she hunched her shoulders and crossed her arms as if to say 'Don't you dare come anywhere near me!' But Cassie was in a good mood and she was sure that Freya couldn't be as bad as she looked, so she went over to her.

'What's up?' she said, sitting on the arm of her chair.

Freya gave her a scathing look.

'What, just because I don't particularly feel like dancing to rubbish music and my dorm has been invaded by a load of badly-dressed weirdos?'

Cassie laughed.

'I suppose you've got a point. It's not really my thing either, but Daisy's so cool and she deserves a good party.'

Freya just humphed in response and looked away.

'Oh well, have fun!' beamed Cassie as she turned away to join the others.

Somehow, even though she was openly rude, Freya didn't bother her in the same way that Tara did.

Tara was dancing along with all the others, but in a snaky-hipped way as if she was twenty-five not twelve. Plus she always had one eye on the mirror and kept looking at the door as if a talent-scout or a paparazzi photographer might burst through it at any moment. When they were all danced out, Daisy shouted, 'Come on, let's do make-up!'

They all tried to squeeze in front of the one full-length mirror as they plastered each other in make-up, and then Bella took control of Megan's video camera and they took turns to walk down an imaginary catwalk and do some kind of silly performance at the end. Only Tara took it seriously, of course, treating them all to a full-length performance of 'I feel pretty' from *West Side Story*.

'I would do a dance,' she explained, 'but we all know who the best dancer is and I wouldn't want to steal the show.'

'What's her problem with me?' whispered Cassie to Bella, whilst Tara was singing her song.

'Oh, she used to be Princess Octavia's favourite last year and you've kind of taken her place I think,' Bella whispered back.

Bella was next on the catwalk, striding confidently to the front and launching into her own rendition of *Daisy, Daisy, give me your answer do*, but with slightly ruder words. She ended up on her knees, 'proposing' to Daisy with a plastic flower ring which she produced from behind her back, and with which she proceeded to squirt Daisy in the eye. Both Jasmine and Freya refused to join in the catwalk show: Freya out of grumpiness and Jasmine out of shyness.

'Come on,' urged Bella, 'you're a dancer for goodness' sake! Just give us a twirl.'

'I can't,' Jasmine wailed, 'not with you all watching.'

'So, you're just going to be a secret ballerina?' teased Bella 'Only dancing when no one's watching?'

'No, it's different on a proper stage. I don't feel like *me* then. But here, with you all watching … well, I can't just do the whole silly thing, and I can't exactly do a proper serious dance, can I?'

'It's fair enough,' said Cassie. 'Why should we all be show-offs? Leave her alone.'

So Bella moved on to Freya, but the look she gave her, which was more a growl than a look, made her give up pretty quickly. Flo, on the other hand, decided she *would* do a dance and entertained them all with her unique blend of street, tap and 'ballet', performed completely out of time to the tune of *Dancing Queen*. Then just as she was dropping into a final curtsey, she trod on the end of her feather boa, clattered into the food table and fell backwards onto Tara, who spilt her Coke-float all down her dress and all over the carpet. It was at this point that Bella decided to call time on the party. They finished up by scoffing all the food – or as much of it as wasn't squashed into the carpet – and then a few minutes before lights out, the Fonteyn girls called out their goodbyes and raced back to their own dorm.

True to her promise, Cassie snuck back to Hepburn after lights out to help Flo clear up the mess. When she opened the door, Flo was kneeling on the floor looking forlornly at the Coke stain. The room was still looking very much as if it had just held a raucous party, except that most of its inhabitants were now fast asleep. Cassie dropped down to the floor, and they both scrubbed furiously at the carpet with their flannels, whilst Flo, who was terrified that Cassie would get caught, chattered away nervously like some Beatrix Potter mouse character:

'Oooh, you should really get back,' she whispered urgently. 'Don't worry about this, it's my fault. I'll clear it up. Oh, please don't get in trouble again, I can't bear it.'

'Oh, Flo! Shut up!' said Cassie, 'we'll be done in a minute.'

They laid a towel over the wet stain and stamped on it, then crammed all the paper plates and cups and stray bits of food into plastic bags, which they tied up tightly and squashed into the bin. When it was all done, Cassie finally gave in to Flo's anxious pleas and agreed to go back to her own dorm. She poked her head out of the door to check that the corridor was clear, then made a dash for it and reached her room in safety, slightly disappointed that she hadn't run into any teachers on the way.

The next morning, Cassie was feeling so tired from all the dancing and laughing and carpet scrubbing of the night before that she decided to stay in bed. Stuffing her head under the pillow, she resolutely ignored the calls of the others urging her to get up, and stayed in bed throughout breakfast and into the first lesson. She had asked Jasmine to say she wasn't very well, so she wasn't too surprised to hear the bedroom door opening at around ten am, but she *was* surprised to see when she peered over the top of her duvet that her visitor was Mrs Frost.

'Cassandra,' she said, whisking back the curtains and forcing open the window to let in an icy breeze. 'You have unfortunately missed approximately thirty five minutes of your history lesson, so you will need to catch that work up in my office after school.'

She swept over to the wardrobe, then back to the bedside, giving Cassie a polite, forced smile as she handed over her uniform.

'There we are,' she said, checking her watch, 'now if you hurry, you'll be just in time for French and then you won't be forced to spend any further time in my office this afternoon.'

And before Cassie knew it, the door had clicked closed and she was putting on her uniform.

'Seriously?' Cassie moaned to Flo later on at break, 'Does there *have* to be an exactly equal and opposite punishment for every little misdemeanour? Doesn't the woman have an ounce of imagination?'

'I think you got away lightly,' said Flo. 'I can't imagine daring to stay in bed.'

Cassie had yawned her way through French and English, and by the time it came to afternoon dance lessons, she was just about ready to give up and lie down. As they walked into the dance studio, she slapped her cheeks a few times in an attempt to wake herself up. Princess Octavia saw her and commented, 'That is a good idea, freckle girl, give yourself a few slaps now in case you misbehave later.'

There were a few sniggers around the room, but Cassie didn't mind. She had got used to Princess Octavia's rudeness by now, and actually found her quite funny. She just sat down and slipped on her shoes, loving the way the scuffed satin instantly became part of her foot, as if it had been incomplete before. She stepped into the chalk box, enjoying the familiar rough scratch of her feet on the floor as she walked away, and began to bend and stretch in preparation for the lesson. Her spirits lifted as her body came alive, and after a few minutes she felt completely awake, as if normal life was hibernation and dancing was Spring.

Three claps rang out like bullet shots around the room and they all skipped over to the *barre* to adopt positions, but almost as soon as the lesson had started, Princess Octavia launched into one of her wistful reminiscences. The girls always knew they were coming because she would sit on her high stool and stare off into a corner of the ceiling as her voice rose to an operatic wobble.

'As my dear friend Voltaire used to say, "Dancing is an art because it has rules". All forms of art exist only because of rules. Indeed, my cherished pupil Margot Fonteyn once said that self-expression is only possible through rules.'

She assumed correctly that none of the girls knew that

Voltaire was a French writer who had died in 1778, and that she had never met Margot Fonteyn.

'It is very well having fine ideas of being dancer,' she continued, 'but the body is naturally lazy and would rather learn wrong movements because they are at first easier. So all the time we must correct it and make it learn right position. A dancer perfects her positions all her life, from little girl to old lady.'

She walked over to Tara, who adopted her best posture.

'This girl here has most graceful *port de bras* – her arms look as if they are floating on air.'

Tara beamed and her sleek, white-blonde hair seemed to sparkle even more brightly. Then Princess Octavia continued, 'It is shame her core is weak because she concentrates too much on being pretty. Now, *plies*.'

The girls all took hold of the *barre* again and Cassie noticed how Tara, who was two places in front of her, looked lovingly at the graceful curve of her own arm.

'First position. Good. Second position. The girl with boy's hair needs to turn her right foot towards the mirror slightly. Third position.' She walked up and down the line and the girls almost buzzed with the effort to be correct. 'Fourth position. Watch that back foot you who giggles too much.' She tapped the girl in question, just to make sure she knew who she was.

They performed six *demi-plies* and six *grand-plies* in each position, then moved on to variations of arm and body movements, bending to each side, arching backwards, raising their legs, all without altering the fixed stance of their hips. It was difficult work and Princess Octavia pushed them hard, never letting any slip pass unnoticed. The quiet of the room was frequently broken by her sharp-pointed words: 'Lift that arm! Not floppy like a toy rabbit.' 'Too far down! You want to lick the floor?' 'Are you a tree? Too stiff. Loosen!' When they performed the *rond de jambe*, drawing semi-circles with their pointed foot, first on the floor, then in the air, Princess Octavia called everyone's attention to Cassie's body, 'You see her hips – turned right out – beautiful!'

After that, they moved into the middle of the room to practise jumps, pirouettes and point-work. This was the area where Tara excelled most. In the *grand jeté*, she could leap into the air in beautiful arcs as if she were a fairy painting rainbows. Even Cassie had to admit that as you watched her rising, soaring and falling gracefully like the most perfect ballerina doll the world has ever seen, you couldn't help but smile. It was such a beautiful sight.

At the end of the lesson, as the girls were dropping to the floor, red-faced and breathless, to take off their shoes, Princess Octavia surprised them by throwing out casually: 'So, we perform *The Nutcracker* in six weeks' time.'

They had all been aware that there would be an end of term performance, but no one had known so far what it would be, and anyone who had presumed to ask had been brusquely hushed. Now they were all silent in anticipation.

'Not the full ballet, of course, you are not good enough for that, but a short one arranged especially by myself for little ones. I will audition you when you come back from half-term holiday. Of course, every girl wishes to be the star, but only one will be the star.'

Princess Octavia's face cranked into a smile and she looked around at them all, seeming pleased about the misfortune which would befall everyone else.

'We will have to work very hard – after school very much and weekends as well as school days. It will be hard, hard work,' she nodded with a satisfied grin. 'You are dismissed.'

After class, the changing room was bursting with excitable chatter.

'Tara will play Clara, of course,' whispered most of the Year 7 girls, looking at her in adoration. But Tara herself was smugly silent. She only narrowed her eyes to look like a mysterious exotic princess and smiled knowingly, 'Who is going to play my nutcracker prince? That's what I'd like to know.'

Chapter 5: *Fun and Games*

It took Cassie a while to plot her revenge on Mrs Frost and Starlight Academy in general – partly because she was so busy dancing, and partly because she was in two minds about how far she should go. She thought of weeing in the moat as an act of defiance against the uniform perfection of the whole place, but no one would know apart from the fish, and it didn't seem fair on them – *they* couldn't help it if they were neat and perfect. She thought of dyeing her hair red, and painting her face grey, as a statement of protest against the absurd rigidity of 'school colours', but she didn't actually want to get thrown out of the school and she sensed she might be pushing Mrs Frost too far. So she did the next best thing, and one night after dinner, she took the packet of red hair dye she had bought in one of her bolder moments, crept outside to the fountain in the entrance courtyard, and tipped the contents of it into the water. It made her feel so good to do it, she couldn't help giggling to herself at the thought of the immaculate fountain spurting messy blood-red water. But once she had started, she couldn't stop. She looked around at the pristine courtyard and decided to tackle the smugly symmetrical stones in the gravel drive. So breaking a stick off one of the thick ivy

57

bushes, she painstakingly scratched a message into the dirt beneath the stones: **STRAITJACKET ACADEMY** she wrote in large, clear letters. It gave her such a ruffle of pleasure to look at the dishevelled stones. But then, out of the corner of her eye, she saw Mrs Frost walking towards her. She hadn't quite planned for this bit.

*　*　*

In a panic, she threw the stick to one side and tried to rub out the message with her foot, but it didn't work and she didn't have time. Her next instinct was to get down on her knees, as if to be knighted, or beheaded, but the moment passed and she was still on her feet with her hands behind her back and her head hung low when the headmistress reached her. Mrs Frost stood there for a few moments without speaking, but Cassie could hear her calm, measured breaths. She stared hard at the polished toes of the headmistress' shoes for a few more moments, wondering if she could see herself in them, and then slowly she looked up into her eyes. To her surprise, she saw that Mrs Frost was smiling. A small, thin, sideways smile, like a medieval woman in a painting, but a smile nonetheless.

'Cassie, my dear,' she said, shaking her head, 'you're obviously determined to break the rules in one way or another, and in a sense I admire that, but I also think it's plain foolish, and you're no fool. Now what exactly is your difficulty?'

She said it so directly and so kindly that Cassie found herself answering quite honestly and easily.

'I just hate being told what to do all the time. And it

seems like it's just for the sake of it, just to make you feel trapped. What's wrong with thinking for yourself?'

'Nothing at all, my dear, nothing at all. But you are missing the point. Rules are – as you say – in a way just for the sake of it. They are there partly to keep you all in order, of course, and to prevent chaos breaking out. But they are also there simply so that you follow them, because following them will help you to rise above your own personal desires.'

Cassie continued to look at her miserably, so she went about it another way.

'Imagine if you were principal dancer at the Royal Ballet and on your opening night you suddenly felt like wearing jeans and trainers on stage, just because you wanted to. What use would you be if you just went ahead and did what you felt like doing?'

'I suppose so.'

'If you can try to see all these rules as the best training for the wonderful life of performing that lies ahead of you, it might help a bit.'

'But for me the whole point of dancing is to be free, not restricted.'

'You are right. But that is a different kind of freedom and that you will never lose.'

There was something about the way Mrs Frost spoke that made it impossible to doubt the truth of what she said. The headmistress smiled and smoothed down Cassie's hair, just once briefly with her hand. It was what her dad did when she was feeling low and suddenly Cassie no longer felt angry or trapped, she felt calm and happy.

*   *   *

It turned out, as Princess Octavia informed them in the next lesson, that some boys from the Royal Ballet School in London would be shipped in: one to play Fritz and the nutcracker prince, and another to play Uncle Drossellmeyer and the mouse king. They would join the girls for rehearsals after half-term. Everyone was full of the excitement of the performance and Cassie did her best to join in, trying hard to bury her hopeless, urgent desire to play Clara. Because there was no point wishing and hoping, when it was obvious that Tara was older, prettier and more experienced. That night, Cassie rushed straight back to the dorm after dinner so that she could have a few moments alone while everyone else was in the Common Room watching TV. Once safely inside with the door shut, she slid her hand under the bed and took out her mother's ballet shoes. Then she lay back on her bed, held the shoes to her chest, closed her eyes and whispered urgently, 'I *so* want to be Clara. I've never wanted anything so badly. Normally I'm not desperate to be the star, but I've always loved Clara.'

To Cassie, talking to a pair of old ballet shoes didn't seem at all odd because she had been doing it all her life. Besides, in her own mind she wasn't talking to shoes at all but to the mother she had never known. It wasn't a sad, heart-breaking thing like in a weepy film, it was just the way she talked to her mum if she needed to share secrets or sort out problems in her head. But she did realise that to anyone else it would seem completely weird so she made it quick before anyone came back to the room.

'Anyway, I'm going to go for it. I'm going to practise my audition piece all over half-term, and I'm going to get it, I really am.'

She hurriedly put the shoes back in their box and had just stowed them safely under her bed when Bella and Megan burst in.

'I hear you lot are doing *The Nutcracker* at Christmas,' said Bella. 'Fab – especially as it will bring some boys in. That'll cheer up the second half of term.'

Cassie laughed. She wasn't so mad about the whole boy thing as everyone else seemed to be. The only boy she had really known well was Milo and she didn't think of him in that way at all.

'What about the rest of you? Don't the singers and actors put on a show?'

'Well, we all do little bits and pieces – we'll be doing some sketches and scenes and the singers will do a couple of concerts, but yours is the biggy this term. Our major performances will come in the Spring and Summer terms. We don't know what yet, but ours rarely require boys, you see. Girls just play the male parts. You dancers are the lucky ones. You have to have boys to make it work properly.'

'I don't see what the big deal is about boys,' said Megan. 'They're either so full of themselves that they're just dull, or they're painfully shy and won't talk to anyone.'

Just then Jasmine came in with a tray carrying four mugs

of hot chocolate and a plate of biscuits. Her tongue was poking out the corner of her mouth with the effort of keeping all the clanking cups from falling off the tray as she teetered over to her bedside table.

'Jasmine, you're a star!' said Megan. 'How did you manage that?'

'Oh, I was upset about not being in the Sports Tournaments because I'm rubbish at hockey so I haven't been picked for my house team and I didn't get through the tennis heats. It's not that I love sport or anything but I really wanted to do *something* to be part of it. Then Miss Mackenzie caught me coming out of dinner and said "Are you alright, dear?" and you know how that always makes you cry when someone says that, so I burst out crying and she thought it was far worse than it is – because I don't mind *that* much – and took me to her room and gave me hot chocolate and I asked if I could bring some up for you lot.'

She wasn't used to speaking so much and paused for breath.

'Well *we* think you're great, even if you are rubbish at hockey and tennis,' said Bella, giving her a hug, and they all settled down on their beds with their mugs.

'I've got an idea,' said Megan, reaching into her bed-side cabinet and pulling out a pile of magazines. 'The latest instalments from my mum,' she explained, 'she likes to keep me up to date. You lot can read them and I'll carry on with my book, it's got to a really good bit.'

The other three grabbed the magazines eagerly, shared them out and sprawled on their beds to read them.

'Must get an early night, though, if we want to be our best for the try-outs tomorrow,' said Bella, and then waggled her finger and added in Mrs Frost's voice,

'"Discipline, girls, is the key."'

They hadn't been reading for long when Cassie suddenly leant over and grabbed Jasmine's arm, 'Hey, I've just thought – why don't you be my doubles partner in the tennis tournament? It's meant to be Flo but Tara's asked her to be her partner and I know she's desperate to say yes even though she's too loyal to admit it.'

'But I'm much worse at tennis than Flo,' said Jasmine, 'I wasn't going to enter the doubles at all.'

'Oh come on, it'll be fun. I don't care about winning, we can just have a laugh.'

'Alright then,' said Jasmine smiling, 'as long as you don't have a go at me when I miss.'

'OK, promise. We don't have to put our names down until tomorrow morning so I'll talk to Flo about it first thing.'

The morning of the Half-term Tournament was drizzly and overcast, and by the time they had finished breakfast the rain was pelting down.

'Perfect!' said Megan moodily. 'We'll be sliding all over the hockey pitch like demented ice-skaters.'

The school was divided into four houses named after famous theatres: Sadler's Wells, Coliseum, Adelphi and Lyric, and the Year 11 heads of each house were in charge of choosing their hockey teams from across the years. They had to pick at least two girls from each year group and Flo had been chosen as one of the Year 7 team-members for her house, Sadler's Wells, so she was a bundle of nerves all morning. She was delighted to have been chosen, but terrified of letting everyone else in the team down.

'I just *know* I'm going to keep tripping over my laces and everyone else's sticks, I always do,' she wailed to Cassie.

'But you're *good* at hockey,' Cassie reminded her, 'you know you are.'

'If I can keep on my feet I am,' she agreed.

'And if you can keep your hair out of your eyes,' said Cassie, looking anxiously at the mass of blonde frizzy hair flying all over the place. 'Do you want to borrow some hair-clips? School colours, I promise,' she added, laughing.

By mid-morning the rain had stopped and just as the first parents began to arrive, the sun came out. The parents were given tea in a big, striped, circus-style tent which had been put up on the front lawn near the tennis courts, and they stood about chatting while young children got tangled up in their legs and generally knocked over cups of tea and ate too many biscuits. Cassie had flung her arms around her dad as soon as he stepped out of the car, and had only just managed to let go of his jacket sleeve, but now that he was talking to another father about cricket she decided it was time to look around and check out her friends' families. Tara was, as had been predicted, completely ignoring hers. She was standing instead with

Megan's family, hoping that some of their celebrity lifestyle might rub off on her. Megan's mum was tall and slim and amazingly glamorous; Cassie thought she looked like a model. Her dad was wearing a bright pink and navy blue striped suit with long pointed pink suede shoes and a cool hat tipped to one side of his head. And between them stood Megan, as plain and ordinary as could be, but looking very pleased to be with them and talking excitedly without pausing for breath. Jasmine, too, looked delighted to be back with her parents who had brought her new baby brother along, and they all looked adoringly at each other. Bella's parents were talking to Mrs Frost about the history and architecture of the school building. They both had violin cases slung across their backs and as Cassie passed by, Bella whispered to her, 'I can't believe they've brought their instruments. I've *begged* them not to play any music, but they always bring them in case some impromptu entertainment is required.'

Cassie laughed and then she caught sight of Flo who was calling her over.

Flo's mum was just as Cassie had remembered her from the first day. Her hair was flying all over the place with what looked like feathers sticking out here and there, her clothes were mismatched and home-made looking, and she kept staring around as if she had lost something. As it turned out, she had.

'Have you seen Tom anywhere?' she kept asking Flo.

'No, Mum. He came with you in the car, so I thought you might know where he was. I haven't seen him yet.'

'He must have scurried off somewhere. Wait here, Flo darling, and I'll see if I can find him.'

'Probably practising his bowling somewhere,' she called after her mum, then turned to Cassie, 'Tom's a mad cricketer – the star player at his school. Typical that Mum manages to rescue hundreds of chickens from battery cages every week but keeps losing her own children.'

'That's amazing,' said Cassie, 'I didn't know she did that. That's really cool. Are you allowed to just take them?'

'No. It's the ones that have stopped laying eggs, that are no use to the farmer any more. She and her friends rescue them and nurse them back to health, you know, let them live out the rest of their lives in more comfort and all that. I suppose it is cool of her really, but you get kind of sick of it when the house is full of chicken poo and you can't sleep because of all the squawking. Here's Tom.'

Tom came over, not looking too pleased at having been found. He had lots of straw-coloured hair, mostly in his eyes, which were a sparkling blue. Cassie suddenly felt fidgety, as if she wanted to be somewhere else, but also as if she didn't want to leave.

'Throwing balls around as usual,' explained Flo's mum.

'This is one of my brothers – Tom – probably the least awful one,' explained Flo.

Cassie managed to say 'Hi' but then couldn't think of anything else to say. Flo suddenly ran off to get Tara, and her mum wandered off to get a drink, so Cassie was left standing with Tom.

'So you like cricket?'

'Yup.'

'Are you good?'

'Yup.'

'So you've already broken up for half-term.'

'Yup.'

'Lucky you.'

'Well, you're breaking up today, aren't you?'

'Yes, I suppose so. What year are you in?'

'Nine. Why?'

'I don't know.'

He put his hands in his pockets and looked around with a frown, 'I'm starving. Where's the food in this place?'

Just then Tara came over, and for the first time in her life Cassie was pleased to see her. But a moment later she had a new and unpleasant feeling: for the first time in her life, she wished that she looked like Tara instead of herself.

The Tennis Tournament was first. There had been heats all week and the Tournament consisted of semi-finals and finals for lower school and upper school, and then mixed lower and upper doubles. Cassie was playing against a Year 8 girl called Phoebe in the semis. Phoebe was alarmingly muscular with a fierce look in her eyes, and she never smiled once, but Cassie had been playing tennis with her dad since she was about three and she easily beat her. Before the final, she went to watch the end of the other semi, which featured Tara and a Year 9 girl called Antonia. At first they had been evenly matched and had consistently won their own games but failed to break the other's serve. But when they were half an hour into the match, Antonia broke Tara's serve, went on to win her own game and then broke Tara's serve again. Before long, she was one set up, at which point Tara dropped her racket and flopped dramatically to the ground. There was a gasp from the crowd.

'She's fainted!' several girls cried out in awe.

Flo gripped Cassie's arm and looked at her wide-eyed and horror-stricken, 'Poor Tara!'

'She *would* faint,' said Cassie. 'I just knew she would be a fainter.'

Most of the girls secretly thought 'Lucky her!' and they looked on with envy as the sports mistress, Miss Hurley, and Tara's parents rushed onto the court. But as soon as her parents arrived on the tennis court, Tara made an immediate recovery, sat up, and allowed herself to be escorted from the scene between her father and Miss Hurley. Since Antonia was ahead she was counted the winner, but it wasn't nearly such a blow to Tara as if she really *had* won.

So Cassie now faced Antonia in the finals. She was re-lieved it wouldn't be Tara – one rivalry between them was enough – but she didn't stand a chance against Antonia Du Pont. Antonia was the lower school's hockey cap-tain, and she would have been a tennis pro if she hadn't decided to devote her time to music instead. She was one of those girls who would always be best at every-thing. She was not only musically gifted, but also brainy, pretty and sporty all rolled into one – and somehow nice as well, so you couldn't dislike her for it. The visiting families sat on garden chairs around the tennis court and the girls squeezed themselves onto the wet grassy patches between them to watch the final. Cassie didn't hold out much hope, but she gave it her best. The match was hard-going, but after thirty minutes of playing they were pretty even. By then, Cassie was exhausted, whilst Antonia looked as if she was only just getting started. By the start of the second set she was still skipping lightly around the court as if she was just warming up, and by the end of the second set she had won the game.

Antonia gave Cassie a big friendly smile as she strode up to the net to shake her hand,

'Well done,' she beamed, 'I found that quite hard and I don't often say that.' Then she whispered, 'I don't know how you managed not to faint in this sweltering heat.'

Cassie laughed and as she walked off the court, she couldn't help feeling pleased that the best player had won. She went straight over to her dad who gave her a big hug and then Flo came over dragging her mum and brother behind her.

'Wasn't she amazing?' she kept saying to them.

'Yes fabulous, darling, fabulous,' said Flo's mum absent-mindedly, as if she wasn't quite sure who they were talking about or what they had done.

'She wasn't bad,' said Tom. 'But she didn't win you know,' he pointed out, as if Flo perhaps hadn't noticed.

'I know that, stupid! But no one beats Antonia Du Pont at anything. She was amazing even to get into the final.'

'And not to faint, I guess,' agreed Tom.

Just then Antonia breezed past them, 'Come on, you lot, time for lunch and then it's the house hockey matches,' she said with relish.

'She hasn't even got red cheeks,' said Flo in a voice hushed with awe.

By the end of the hockey matches, which Sadler's Wells won, all the girls – including those just watching – were covered from head to toe in mud, and they were sent off to shower and change into home clothes. Flo was so delighted she hadn't ruined the match for her house and had even managed to stay on her feet for most of the game, that she jumped around and fell backwards into a prickly gorse bush. When they came back out, the sun was just beginning to set and a huge bonfire had been lit on the side lawn. Cassie was wearing her jeans and silver Converse and a bright red woollen hoody poncho, which her dad had brought back from Mexico, plus the purple bandana in her hair and her big turquoise hoop earrings. Flo had insisted on wearing her silver silk dress with her pink feather boa, but, ever practical, she had kept her wellies on because of the mud and was wearing her school mac for warmth.

'Do I look like a film-star?' she asked Cassie hopefully.

'Well, sort of depends which film you're talking about,' said Cassie tactfully, because she secretly thought Flo looked most of all like the scarecrow from the Wizard of Oz, and she wasn't very good at lying.

Now the family games began: there was apple-bobbing, a coconut shy, a three-legged race and a tug of war. There was a terrible moment when Cassie was almost teamed with Flo's brother for the three-legged race, but at the last minute Flo reappeared and took her place, so she pulled out and thankfully watched her dad and Flo's mum hobble about instead. By the end of the games, most of the parents were also covered in mud from falling over so much, and they gathered around the bonfire to eat baked potatoes wrapped in foil and sausages in buns. Cassie and her dad sat with Flo's and Jasmine's families, all of them talking and laughing happily together. The bonfire crackled and the smoke rose up into the air, and as Cassie followed its trail up into the red night-sky, she felt so content that she wondered how she could ever have wanted to leave this place.

Chapter 6: *A Misunderstanding*

When they came back after Half-term, all the dancers were more excited than ever about the upcoming performance of *The Nutcracker*. Auditions were due to be held at the end of the week, but the way everyone talked, it was already decided that Tara would be playing Clara.

'Tara Clara – it even rhymes!' they giggled gleefully, as if it was all so perfect that it was just meant to be.

Cassie couldn't believe that no one else even wanted to give it a go. Or maybe they did and like her were keeping quiet. She found that she couldn't concentrate on anything because her mind was constantly playing over different scenarios, first of Tara getting the part and then of *her* getting the part. She could think of nothing else. In the morning art lesson on the second day back, Miss Chivers had to keep calling her attention back to the arrangement of jars they were supposed to be drawing.

'It's not out of the window, Cassie,' she said, drumming her bony forefinger on the table and rattling the arrangement of jars, 'it's there on the table in front of you.'

Cassie found art one of the most painful subjects. Art teachers always went on about how every artistic creation was important and good in its own way, but it wasn't true. Some people were good at art and some people weren't – the same as anything else – and try as she might, Cassie just couldn't make the jars look round. They looked like jars but they appeared flat, whilst Flo's, for example, were proper round jars.

'Right! Pencils down.'

Miss Chivers' voice broke into her thoughts as she looked one last time at her flat jars and sighed.

'Now we're all going to share our work and learn from each other. Jasmine, could you start us off and hold yours up.'

Oh no, not Jasmine, thought Cassie.

'I can't Miss Chivers, mine's awful, it really is. I'm terrible at art,' wailed Jasmine, blushing crimson.

'You mustn't say that, Jasmine, it simply isn't true. Each drawing has its own worth and merit.'

There she goes, thought Cassie and she must have raised her eyebrows by mistake because Miss Chivers shot her an angry look.

'Except perhaps that *yours* Cassie is more likely to be a drawing of the clouds than these jars,' she said with a sting in her voice. 'Now come on, Jasmine, everyone is going to show theirs and *someone* has to start so it might as well be you.'

Jasmine was beginning to sound tearful, 'Oh, please choose someone else to go first,' she pleaded quietly.

But Miss Chivers had lost patience by now and she almost spat, 'For goodness' sake just get on with it!'

Suddenly, there was a clatter as Jasmine's drawing

board fell to the floor and she ran crying from the room. A ripple of concerned whispers went around the room before Miss Chivers clapped her hands for silence and said with a sigh of exasperation, 'Right, now who *is* prepared to show us their work without bursting out crying?'

Abigail Rowan rose to her feet with a shrug saying, 'I don't mind,' and held up her drawing of the jars.

As they left the art room, Cassie was feeling decidedly irritable.

Poor Jasmine, she thought to herself. *And just when she was beginning to get more confident. What's wrong with everyone at this school? Why can't they just leave people alone once in a while?*

As they jostled along the corridor, Cassie turned to Flo and said, 'What's her problem? What's the big deal about holding up your work?'

Abigail, who was standing nearby, overheard her and butted in loudly, 'Don't be so mean, Cassie. Jasmine's just shy.'

Suddenly everyone seemed to be listening, and others joined in, 'Yeah, poor Jasmine.'

'Exactly, how would *you* like it?'

'She can't help it.'

But before Cassie had time to explain herself, she heard her name being called out from somewhere further down the corridor.

'Hey, dancing queen!' came a jeering voice. 'Or sorry, is it dancing king?'

Tara was walking down the corridor towards them, her hips swaying from side to side, her glossy ponytail swinging in time to her careless swagger. The Year 7 girls all stopped and stared at her in silent admiration.

'Princess Octavia wants to see you in the dance studio,' she continued, unabashed by all the admiring eyes. 'It's about your audition piece apparently.' She let out a brief, barely noticeable, snigger. 'Anyway, what's all the fuss about?'

'Oh, Cassie was just bad-mouthing Jasmine,' Abigail chirped eagerly. 'About her getting so embarrassed all the time.'

'I was *not*!' Cassie protested vehemently. 'I was …'

'I'd hurry up if I were you,' said Tara, slinging her a sideways look. 'Princess O is waiting for her darling puppy dog.'

And suddenly everyone had disappeared, following helplessly in the wake of Tara's swinging ponytail, leaving Cassie to explain to thin air, 'I didn't mean *Jasmine*, I meant Miss Chivers.'

Only Flo was still standing by her side and Cassie turned to her,

'Why do they think I would say that about Jasmine?' she asked defensively. 'She's my friend.'

'I don't know. I guess everyone knows how you can be a bit impatient with people, and how you like to speak your mind,' Flo said. 'They must have just jumped to the wrong conclusion.'

At break time, the talk amongst the dancers was all of

Tara/Clara and which of the boys that had turned up from the Royal Ballet School would be her nutcracker prince. At their brief meeting in the studio, Princess Octavia had urged Cassie to audition for the part of Clara, but she hadn't exactly inspired her with confidence when she added with a mean glint in her eye, 'It is important for those who are sure of getting the part to feel a little the prickle of competition.'

And now she had to witness the spectacle of the all the Year 7 dancers simpering around Tara and hanging off her every word. Suddenly Cassie could bear it no longer. She was feeling in a hot temper and didn't want to risk saying anything she would regret. And besides, she needed to talk to someone about all of this, but who? Her classmates seemed to think she only ever spoke to make nasty comments about people.

So, in the fifteen minutes before the next lesson, she rushed up to the dorm, took out her mother's old ballet shoes from their box under the bed, and poured out her troubles.

'Oh I *wish* I didn't want the part so badly. It's much easier not wanting anything, then you don't get disappointed. I can't decide whether it's better to forget all about it and wait for another year, or to try for Clara. Because I can't bear it if I try and everyone knows I've tried, and I still don't get it.'

She looked at her watch. She had decided after her talk with Mrs Frost never to be late for anything again, so she finished what she had to say in a hurry, 'Why can't I just accept that Tara is the better dancer for the part? I mean I bet Clara doesn't have short boyish hair and millions of freckles. It would be so much easier just to be a mouse, or a sweet, or a tea-cup.'

Then she shoved the shoes back in their box and leapt down the stairs two at a time to get to French on time.

As soon as she walked into the classroom, Cassie realised something was wrong. Everyone turned to look at her with cold eyes and she saw that Jasmine was quietly weeping in the corner, with a huddle of girls around her saying comforting things. As Cassie was staring around in confusion her eye was caught by something on the white-board and she looked over to see the two lines of big blue writing:

Q: What's the difference between Jasmine and a traffic light?
A: A traffic light only goes red some of the time.

Her heart leapt into her throat. What a horrible thing to write. Who did it? Her temper rose in defence of her friend. Then suddenly it dawned on her, and her whole body went icy cold in an instant.

'What, you think *I* wrote it?' she said in disbelief to her class.

'Obviously,' said a quiet, mean voice from the crowd.

'But Jasmine's my friend – aren't you, Jasmine?' she pleaded. 'Why would I write something so horrible about her? I wouldn't even think it.'

But Jasmine wouldn't look at her and Cassie began to feel a sense of despair creeping up her body.

Just then Madame Hugo came into the room. She took one look at the board and the scene, tutted sadly with a shake of her head, and then looked around accusingly. Madame Hugo was not the kindliest of teachers. Her face was crooked, with one eye noticeably higher than the other, and she had a cruel sense of humour, often sharing private jokes with herself in French, which the girls were sure made fun of them.

'*Asseyez-vous, s'il vous plait,*' she said crossly and they sat obediently. Then she babbled in French for a bit, shaking her head and narrowing her eyes at each of them in turn, as if they were all equally as bad as each other. Suddenly, she broke into English, 'Before I take the matter to Madame Frost, the 'orrible girl who wrote it has one chance to own up and get her misery out of the way now.'

There was a chilling silence and Cassie felt the eyes spiking into her.

'So be it,' said Madame Hugo after a painfully long wait. 'Let Mrs Frost pinch it out of you instead.'

The lesson was agonisingly long and Cassie heard none of it. Her stomach was churning and accusing voices were ringing in her head. *How could they think it was her? Was she that nasty? Was that really how they all saw her?* There was a painful lump in her throat but she was too numb to cry. It was a relief when finally the bell went and she could attempt to clear her name.

'Well, where *were* you then?' asked Abigail, taking charge in a hard, unforgiving voice.

Lauren joined in:

'Yeah. At break time you ran off. Where did you go?'

Cassie hesitated. How on earth would she explain it?

'I just needed some time on my own, to work a few things out, so I went up to my room.'

'How convenient,' said Abigail to the others. Cassie could have hit her.

'I *did*, it's true.'

But she knew that no matter how many times she said it, no one was going to believe her, because Jasmine wouldn't even look at her, let alone talk to her.

By lunchtime, everyone seemed to have heard about it and she noticed several Year 8 girls looking at her coldly too. Tara seemed to have taken Jasmine under her wing and was walking everywhere with her arm around her. When Cassie tried to talk to her, Tara steered her away and said to Jasmine, 'Don't worry, just ignore her.'

The rest of that day was the most miserable of Cassie's life. If she had thought she was unhappy when she first arrived at Starlight, it was nothing compared to this. In the dorm that evening, she didn't dare speak and tried not to look at anyone. It wasn't difficult because Jasmine was completely avoiding her eyes and Megan and Bella didn't seem to have anything much to say to her either. She felt that it was pointless trying to explain herself and went to bed as quickly as she could. Only once the lights were out did the tears finally pour out onto her pillow.

Chapter 7: *The Poison Pen Strikes Again*

The next morning on the way down to breakfast, Cassie managed to get hold of Flo before they reached the dining hall.

'Can we talk quickly?' she asked hurriedly.

'Of course,' said Flo with a warm smile.

They stood in a corner on one of the landings and let everyone else stream past them. Flo was the first to speak, 'It's horrible, all this stuff. Poor you.'

'I have to know,' demanded Cassie in an urgent voice. 'Do you believe it wasn't me?'

Flo laughed, 'Of course it wasn't you! Don't be silly. You wouldn't do something like that.'

Cassie was so relieved that she almost cried again. At last, a chink of light had appeared in her dark tunnel.

'Then how can I persuade everyone else?' she asked.

Flo took a creased sheet of music out of her pocket and rescued a short stubby pencil from her bird's nest of hair and began to scribble some notes.

'Well, first of all,' she said, detective style 'what *were* you doing when it happened?'

Cassie thought for a moment.

'OK, I think I can tell you,' she decided. 'You know how my mum died when I was really young and she was a dancer too. Well, I have a pair of her old ballet shoes and I sort of talk to them like they're her. And that's what I was doing. I came up to the room to talk to my mum's ballet shoes.'

Flo tipped her head to one side and bit her lip as if she was about to cry.

'Look don't get all drippy about it, it's fine. It's not a sad thing. It's just something I've always done. Well anyway, that was what I was doing, talking to her, but I couldn't exactly say that because it makes me sound like a loony.'

Flo rubbed her chin thoughtfully, 'Hmm … and you can't even tell them that now, because everyone would just think you were making it up. What were you talking to her about anyway?'

'Oh, just the auditions for *The Nutcracker* and how I really want to be Clara but I don't know whether to try out for the part or not.'

They were walking down to the dining hall now, but Flo stopped and turned to face Cassie:

'Why on earth wouldn't you?'

'Because then if I don't get the part, everyone will think I'm disappointed and feel sorry for me and I couldn't bear it.'

'But you *would* be disappointed.'

'Of course I would, but I don't want everyone to know it.'

Flo frowned as if she were trying to work out a tricky

puzzle, 'So instead, you'd rather audition to be a tea-cup or something and then when you get it everyone will think you're really pleased.'

Cassie laughed. It was such a relief to laugh.

'Well, when you put it like that it sounds a bit ridiculous.'

'Exactly. So you're going to audition for Clara, right?'

'I guess so.'

By now they had reached the hall, which was bursting with the clatter of breakfast, so Flo quickly got back to the main issue.

'But listen, we haven't solved your problem yet.'

'I know. I almost forgot about it for a moment there.'

'Well, as I see it, the only way we can convince everyone that it wasn't you, is by finding out who it really was.'

'But how?'

'No idea.'

They went into breakfast talking it over, and Cassie felt that she might actually be able to eat something, because everything was no longer quite so completely bleak.

As soon as breakfast was over, however, Mrs Frost called their entire form together to talk to them, and Cassie found that she felt just as sick and miserable and frightened as she had the day before. Mrs Frost did her best not to look at Cassie while she was talking, but she still felt as if she was standing in court with a spotlight on her.

'Girls, Madame Hugo has told me about the unpleasant incident in your classroom yesterday. You know, of course, that I will not tolerate any form of bullying whatsoever in this school, and to humiliate a girl in that way is an act of cruelty I take extremely seriously. I am also aware of the rumours circulating about who is responsible, but I will not judge a girl on mere hearsay and gossip. Either the girl responsible can come to my study by the end of the day, or I will be forced to launch a thorough investigation.'

She looked closely at every girl to check that the message had been understood, and then said, 'That is all, you may go.'

Cassie rushed out of the room first because she couldn't bear to look any of her classmates in the eye and see what they were thinking. She was going to head straight out of the front door and run as fast as she could, but she changed her mind, went back to the dorm to get her shoes and leotard, and went instead to one of the rehearsal rooms. For the half hour before classes started, she practised her audition piece and for those few precious minutes, she lost herself in the wide-open freedom of dancing. It was as if she entered another bigger world where no one judged her and nothing that normally mattered seemed the slightest bit important. She left the dance studio feeling carefree and happy. She was sure it would all get sorted out and people would realise soon enough that she had had nothing to do with the malicious attack on Jasmine. She changed quickly back into her uniform and went to the classroom for English.

* * *

Mrs Wade had her box of interesting things out on the table, which meant that they would be doing creative writing. She whisked around the room, throwing open windows with gusto and taking in deep breaths of the freezing air that billowed in, 'Ah! Wonderful! Breathe in that creative force, girls! Deep, delicious breaths!'

Mrs Wade was always in an amazingly good mood. Nothing ever seemed to dampen her cheerful attitude to life.

'Just feel that air filling your body and feeding the creative impulse,' she urged, wafting the air into the room as if she was conducting an orchestra. The girls all went along with her breathing exercises quite happily because her enthusiasm was so infectious. Then she went over to her box and began handing out old black-and-white postcards of people. They were caught in various different activities, either posing for the camera, or just going about their daily business.

'Look at your picture for a few minutes,' Mrs Wade instructed. 'Lose yourself in it. Step into the scene. Become one of those people in the picture. Feel what it's like to be them, to have their body and think their thoughts.'

There was silence for a few minutes.

'Now begin to write. Write as that person.'

They all scribbled away for a while and when they had finished, everyone had to read theirs out. Cassie had a photo of three grubby children, a girl and two boys, sitting on a wall, with a woman in the background hanging out washing and looking crossly over her shoulder at them. She had connected immediately with the girl sandwiched between her older brothers on the wall, who looked as if she had just done something naughty. The writing came easily, and she lost herself in the picture so much that she felt almost normal.

Next Mrs Wade took out various objects from the natural world and began to hand them around. There were twigs, shells, fruits, stones, lumps of moss, all sorts of things.

'*Really* connect with your object,' she said, as she went around placing them on the desks, 'touch it, smell it, look at every tiny aspect of it, taste it if you like. Enter into it. Become one with it. Really *feel* what it is like to be it.'

There were a few giggles around the room as girls licked moss, and stuck twigs up their noses, but eventually the room settled down to silence, and then Mrs Wade said again, 'Now write.'

This time she picked girls out randomly to read theirs out.

'Florence. I know you like to call yourself Flo, but when you are named after one of the most exquisite cities in the world, I refuse to call you a name that sounds like a toilet-cleaning product.'

Flo stood up shyly and held up her red maple leaf for all to see. Then she read out:

'*Take a peek
At my bright red leaf*

Like a rosy cheek
Like a feather on an Indian chief
Or a big red star
In the night sky so far.'

'Lovely, Florence!' Mrs Wade clapped her hands in delight. She had a way of making everyone think they were the most fantastic writer ever. 'You have played with rhyme in a wonderfully mischievous, light-hearted way.'

'Have I?' said Flo, pleased with herself.

'Now, Freya.'

Freya stood up but kept her eyes on her desk. She held up her horse-chestnut, still in its spiky green casing, dangling from a bent twig. Then, still without looking up, she read out:

'Stuck in a dark hole
Squashed, squashed,
Can't get out.
Spikes all around me
To keep out the cruel world
When will it end?'

There was silence for a moment, then Mrs Wade said, forcing a smile, 'Thank you dear. That was very … honest.'

Freya sat down in her chair again, and Mrs Wade moved on. Some of the girls raised their eyebrows at each other, as if to say 'Typical Freya', but they had soon forgotten her.

Outside at break time a group of Year 7s stood with a few Year 8 girls shivering in the winter chill.

'You should have heard Freya's poem in English today,' said Abigail, laughing.

'Sshh,' said Flo in a fierce whisper, 'don't be mean. You'd hate it if someone made fun of yours.'

'I know, but it was so typical,' Abigail hooted, imitating Freya's deep voice. 'All doom and gloom and misery.'

'Well, maybe there's a reason why she's like that,' said Jasmine.

'Exactly,' agreed Tara, who had suddenly become Jasmine's best friend overnight. 'Some people are just strange and it's cruel to make fun of them. They can't help it, it's just the way they are.' She looked pointedly at Cassie. 'Nobody's perfect, you know.'

There was an awkward silence in which everyone seemed to look at Cassie – as if it was *her* who had made the mean comments about Freya.

That evening in the Common Room, Cassie sat on her own, picking the foam out of a hole in the sofa arm as she waited for Flo. But Flo had a late flute lesson and she seemed to be taking ages. Meanwhile, everyone around her was either reading, or watching TV, or playing table tennis, or listening to music; none of them asked her to join in. She looked over at Jasmine and Tara, who were huddled together in a corner listening to an ear-phone each of Tara's iPod. Then suddenly she was struck by a brilliant idea. It was Jasmine's birthday at the weekend – she could organise a party for her, like Daisy's! That might prove to her what a good friend she really was. But when she thought about it a bit more, she realised that Jasmine would absolutely hate to have a party where she was the centre of attention and everyone was looking at her.

I know, I'll book cinema tickets instead, she thought, *as a surprise. I'll get tickets for me and her and Flo and get permission to go into town on Saturday afternoon. Then maybe we can talk properly, if I can just get her away from Tara for a few moments.*

She jumped up and left the room, pleased to have found one positive solution to her problems, and went to call the cinema.

The next morning, Cassie woke up feeling sick with nerves. It was the day that Mrs Frost would launch her investigation, unless someone had already owned up, and although she was innocent, she knew she would have to explain herself all over again. Jasmine still couldn't bring herself to look at Cassie as they all dashed around the dorm getting washed and dressed, but Bella and Megan both sent her pitiful smiles, as if in support. Cassie managed to eat a few mouthfuls of breakfast and then, to take her mind off the investigation, decided to practise her audition piece again in the gap before lessons started. After half an hour's dancing, she couldn't help feeling happy again, and she bounded into the classroom for History feeling light-hearted and hopeful. But as soon as she got into the room, a familiar cold wind hit her. All faces turned towards her, and this time there was a crowd gathering around Freya. Cassie looked over at the white-board, filled with dread, and there it was in blue marker pen:

Q: What's the difference between Freya and Mr Happy?
A: Where do you want to start?

'It wasn't me!' she yelled at them. 'Why would I write that?' She was almost choking in her effort to make them believe her. Most of them looked away, and no one actually said anything, but she had already said it herself.

'Well it's a bit convenient that you left the Common Room early last night,' said bossy Abigail, who seemed to have nominated herself as class spokesperson. 'We all saw you sneak out. Where did you go?'

Cassie hesitated for a moment. She had been arranging Jasmine's birthday trip to the cinema of course. Maybe she should just say so. But she couldn't quite bring herself to ruin it all – and now she thought about it, it would just sound fake given that they all thought she and Jasmine were enemies. She had hesitated too long.

'Well?' said Abigail again. 'It's pretty obvious you came down here to write this.'

'I didn't!' protested Cassie furiously. 'Anyway, it's such a lame joke. If I was going to make up rude jokes about people, I would at least make up a better one than that.'

It seemed that everything she said was making it worse and worse. All she wanted to do was run from the room and hide somewhere, but the lesson was about to start and she had decided not to get into trouble about being late anymore, so instead she marched over to the board and rubbed off the two lines of blue writing.

'That's *evidence* actually,' said Abigail, in a sing-song sneer, 'you can't just rub it off.'

'Well I'm not leaving it on there!' said Cassie fiercely. She could feel her temper rising. This was all so unfair! She slammed her school bag down on her desk in a fury. It tipped over, flapped open, and out rolled a blue marker pen. Cassie stared in horror, unable to believe her eyes.

Mrs Frost was quickly informed by a group of girls about the latest insult, and told how the white-board pen had fallen out of Cassie's bag, and after lunch she found herself summoned to the headmistress' office.

'Now Cassie, I have called you in first not because I suspect you, but because yours is the only name which has been mentioned to me in connection with this business and I want to know why that is.'

Cassie didn't know where to start, but being with Mrs Frost made her feel calmer so she took a deep breath and began:

'Well, I know everyone has this idea about me that I say what I think, and sometimes that means I say unkind things, but I don't really mean to, although actually probably I can be a bit nasty sometimes,' she was getting muddled and tried to slow down. 'But then after art I said something that some people overheard, and they thought I was talking about Jasmine, but I wasn't because she's my friend, I really like her. Then I went away early at break, just before the French lesson, but that had nothing to do with it, I just went up to the dorm to … to be on my own for a bit. Then when I came down to the lesson the thing about Jasmine was written on the board and they all think it was me. And now the second message about Freya and somehow the white-board pen got into my bag but I didn't put it there … and I don't know what to do.'

Her voice cracked and she had tears in her eyes, but Mrs Frost didn't try to comfort her. All the time she had been talking, the headmistress had listened in silence without moving her eyes for one moment from Cassie's face, in fact without moving at all, but Cassie couldn't tell from her look what she thought. When she finally spoke, it was in a cool, measured tone:

'I want very much to believe that it was not you, Cassie. I will speak to Jasmine next. You may go now.'

Cassie was trembling by the time she left the office. It was all so serious. What would happen to her if Mrs Frost decided she was guilty? Would she be expelled? What would her dad think? What would he say when he heard about all of this?

Chapter 8: *In the Woods at Night*

By the end of the school day, Cassie felt like a torn and crumpled rag. No one would look at her or speak to her except for Flo, who kept her going with smiles and hugs whenever she saw her. Freya herself didn't seem to mind about what had been written on the board. She had even announced at break in front everyone:

'Look, I couldn't care less what anyone thinks or says about me, it doesn't make any difference.'

But everyone else minded on her behalf, and did their best to make Cassie suffer. Throughout the day, several girls from their class had been called into Mrs Frost's office, but there hadn't been any announcements yet as to who was guilty. To make it even worse, the auditions for *The Nutcracker* were the very next day and Cassie needed to stay calm in order to give herself the best chance.

After dinner, which Cassie hadn't been able to eat, there was still an hour before bedtime when they usually watched TV, played games and chatted, but Cassie didn't want to do any of these things. She couldn't face going into the Common Room, and she couldn't face going up to the dorm until it was time for lights out. But what else could she do? There was only one thing she felt like doing and that was getting as far away from the school as possible. She left the dining hall as soon as she could and headed straight for the back door. The corridors were dark and empty and this time she didn't meet anyone on her way out. The minute she was out of the door, she started running, and didn't stop until she reached the woods surrounding the school. It was pitch black, but Cassie wasn't at all frightened. In fact, she welcomed the blackness because it meant she didn't have to think about anything. She just walked through the woods, smelling deeply the damp, mouldy wood of rotten tree stumps, and listening to the crunch of her feet on the ground, and the scratch and scurry of squirrels up tree trunks.

She wandered aimlessly for a while, treading carefully and holding her arms out in front of her while her eyes got used to the darkness. She made sure that she kept looking back for the strip of purple light where she had come through the gap in the trees. Even though she was about as miserable as it was possible to be, she knew she didn't want to get into any more trouble by getting lost. Suddenly, she realised that she was extremely cold; she had come out in jeans and a thin T-shirt and she was shivering violently. She looked at her watch – eight thirty, it would soon be time to head back, but she wanted to enjoy the quiet of the woods for a few moments longer. She lay down on the damp leaves and looked up, out through the tops of the trees to the endless darkness, where the bright white moon hung still and watchful in the night sky. It made her long to be up there, looking down on all of this as if none of it mattered. She imagined the moon smiling down at her, telling her it would all be alright in the end.

It was quarter to nine – only fifteen minutes until lights out – she had to get back. Cassie kept her eyes on the moon and the glimmering stars clustered around it so that she could stay with its glow of comfort to the last minute, before she was forced back inside. She knew she didn't have much time and she walked quickly, and then started to run. Suddenly her foot got caught on a tree root and she went flying to the ground with a thud. An agonising pain shot through her wrist. She had broken her fall with outstretched hands and now she felt as if shards of glass were stabbing up her arm one after another. The heat of the shock rushed through her body and her heart thumped violently, but she had to get back. She *had* to get back. Having hurt herself would be no excuse – Mrs Frost had made that perfectly clear. In a blur of agony, Cassie managed to force herself to her feet and then she ran for all she was worth, clutching her injured arm tight against her chest in an effort to stop the jolting, blinding pain. She didn't stop running until she was back at school and the door had closed behind her. Then she crept up the stairs to her dorm, weeping quietly, but safe at last. The lights were already out, but she had made it. She had not been caught.

By morning, Cassie's wrist was swollen and red. Her

head throbbed and burnt, and she couldn't stop shaking. She had spent the night in so much pain that silent tears had soaked her pillow, and by morning she couldn't stand it any longer: she would have to go to the sick room. But far worse than the pain during the night had been the awful thought which scratched at her relentlessly, and which she could not escape: the auditions. She would miss the auditions. Matron took one look at her arm and said, 'You won't be going to class today, Cassie. I will let all your teachers know. Sit on the bed, dear.'

Cassie winced as Matron felt around her wrist, before wrapping it in a tight bandage.

'Just a sprain, I think. I'll get the doctor to take a look. But even so it will take some time to heal. You will have to be very careful.'

'The auditions for *The Nutcracker* are today,' began Cassie hopelessly.

Matron shook her head, 'I'm sorry, my dear,' she said. 'You couldn't possibly dance anyway.'

Cassie spent the morning in the sick-room, swamped in misery. The one hope that had kept her going – the slight chance that she might get the part of Clara – was now completely destroyed. Flo came to see her at break time, but even she couldn't cheer her up, and then just before lunch she had another visitor. There was a quiet knock on the door and when Cassie looked up, she was surprised to see Freya standing in the doorway. She was even more surprised to see that she was almost smiling. Freya came over to the bed, 'Hi. I'm really sorry about what happened to you.'

Cassie didn't know what to say. She couldn't believe that Freya was even talking to her, let alone in this kind, gentle voice. Then she carried on, 'I just thought you'd want to know that another message appeared on our classroom board this morning after break.'

At first Cassie wasn't sure what she meant – was she *accusing* her? She was about to defend herself when suddenly it dawned on her what Freya was saying, and she burst out, 'So that means it wasn't me!'

Freya laughed, 'Duh! Yeah, I think so.'

Cassie laughed too in utter relief and gave Freya a one-armed hug.

'But who was the message about?' said Cassie, suddenly realising that someone else's feelings would have been hurt.

'Flo this time. But you know her, I think it went straight over her head. Or she thought it was a compliment or something, because she just laughed.'

'Well, Flo refuses to believe that anyone can be cruel,' said Cassie, 'so she would probably think they meant it nicely somehow. What did it say anyway?'

'Oh, the same old style, *What's the difference between Flo and a scarecrow? A scarecrow can't help it.* Just as hilarious as the others don't you think?' said Freya. 'But anyway, the point is, whoever's been framing you obviously doesn't realise you're in the sick room.'

'Which means,' said Cassie, slowly working it out, 'that it's not someone in our class, because they would all know.'

'Exactly,' said Freya. 'It's obvious, really, who it is.'

'Is it?' said Cassie, momentarily baffled.

'It's Tara, of course. She hates you because you're competition, and she has to make sure you don't get the part of Clara.'

'I know what you mean,' agreed Cassie, 'but it's not *her* fault I ended up in here on audition day. I fell over, she didn't push me.'

'I know that, stupid, but she was probably trying to get you suspended. Or at least so stressed that you couldn't concentrate on dancing.'

'You're right,' said Cassie nodding her head. 'That makes perfect sense. But how on earth are we ever going to prove it?'

Despite the good news, Cassie still had to get through the afternoon knowing that the auditions for *The Nutcracker* would be going on. In afternoon break, she had a visit from Jasmine, who begged her in floods of tears to forgive her for being such a bad friend, then she sat and watched the clock tick past the time when she knew the others would be dancing their audition pieces for Princess Octavia. She felt as if she had eaten a cold potato whole. She wanted to cry, but the tears seemed to be stuck behind the painful potato.

After the end of school, just as it was getting dark, Flo came back into the sick room to see Cassie and did her best to cheer her up by talking at lightning speed about all sorts of things except the audition.

'Oh, guess what? Mum's decided to rescue old cows as well – I know, don't ask! – as long as she doesn't keep them in my bedroom. And Tom has got a cricket scholarship to a new school, but one of my older brothers Gus has been expelled for running away from his school. He says he would have just waited for the holidays and run away from home instead, but nobody would have noticed, so he had to do it from school.'

Cassie broke in suddenly, 'Go on, tell me. Get it over and done with. Tara got the part of Clara didn't she?'

'Yes, I suppose she did, sort of, in a way.'

'What do you mean?'

'Well, she did.'

Cassie's shoulders fell. It was almost a relief now that it was over.

'But, you know, maybe she'll get ill. Or I could – what could I do? – I could poison her – no, too extreme – I know, I could steal her ballet shoes, if you like.'

Cassie laughed, 'No thanks, it's OK. Anyway, you know you could never bring yourself to do something so mean. Besides,' she squeezed Flo's hand, 'you've already done enough just by staying my friend through all of this. It's the only thing that's kept me going.'

They talked about the mystery of the white-board messages and even Flo had to admit that it seemed likely Tara was the culprit, though she didn't like to think it of her.

'We have to work out a way of catching her in the act,' said Cassie. 'That's the only way we're ever going to get the truth out about who's really responsible.'

Chapter 9: *Caught in the Act*

Cassie was out of the sick room the next day with her wrist bandaged, but she wasn't allowed to go to dance classes for the whole of the next week until the sprain had properly healed. She hardly cared about the performance of *The Nutcracker* now. She would probably be given a part in one of the groups of sweets, and she didn't mind which particular sweet it was. It made no difference any more. She was far more concerned about clearing her name once and for all. After much late-night discussion, Cassie, Freya and Jasmine decided to go and see Mrs Frost to tell her about their suspicions. But when they got into her office and stood in front of her desk, they were surprised to find that she wasn't much interested in what they had to say.

'I'm very glad to find that it's unlikely you're to blame, Cassie, but by accusing Tara you are doing just what others have done to you. It's just as unfair. You have no more reason to accuse her than others had to accuse you.'

They left her office feeling slightly ashamed, but just as sure that Tara was the culprit. That evening, they met again in their dorm to work out a plan. Bella and Megan were there too and they agreed to help find out if it really was Tara writing the cruel messages.

'We have to catch her in the act,' said Megan, 'that's the only way of actually proving it.'

'Which means,' agreed Bella, 'that we have to get her to do it again. We have to get her to write another spiteful comment and then catch her doing it.'

'But then what?' said Jasmine. 'Unless Mrs Frost actually sees her with her own eyes, it's just our word against Tara's.'

Cassie had her doubts too.

'If we're going to drag Mrs Frost along to witness it, we'd have to be pretty sure we were right. And besides, how on earth are we going to make Tara do it again? She hasn't got a reason to any more: she got the part; I'm not a threat.'

'Maybe she doesn't need you out of the way so urgently,' Megan pointed out, 'but she still doesn't like you, so if we give her another easy opportunity to make you more enemies, she won't be able to help herself.'

'I've got it!' yelled Bella, giggling with excitement. 'We'll use *me*. You can make a mean comment about me – like about me being fat or something – we have to make sure you say it in front of Tara and that lots of other people hear. And then we just have to give her an easy opportunity to go to the Year 8 classroom in break to write the message on the board and we can catch her coming out.'

They were all silent for a while, thinking about it.

'It *could* work,' said Cassie, awkwardly. 'But I don't

really want to say anything about you being fat, because I don't think you are.'

'Oh, I don't mind' said Bella, waving if off. 'I'm not the kind of girl who needs to be stick-thin to like myself. I'm pretty happy with my body,' she said, doing a model-pose in the mirror and blowing herself a kiss.

'If it's the only way we can find out if Tara really is the one,' said Flo anxiously, 'then I suppose we'll have to do it. Who knows? It might not even be her after all.'

Once they had planned carefully what to do, it all worked quite smoothly. At break time the next day, Bella made sure that she took two buns and when she came over to join the group of girls huddled by the roaring fire in the dining hall, she winked at Cassie and began to stage the exchange that they had prepared.

'God, I'm starving!' began Bella, wolfing down her bun. 'I'm always hungrier in winter. Sort of like a hiber-nating animal.'

'I didn't know elephants hibernated,' said Cassie.

There was a shocked silence. Even Jasmine, Freya and Megan, who were in on the plan, looked at Cassie in horror. In fact, even Cassie herself felt horrified at what she had been forced to say, but she kept up the act.

'Sorry – but I'm only saying what everyone else is thinking,' she said defensively.

'*I* certainly wasn't thinking that,' said Megan.

'No, me neither,' several others agreed.

'Only *you* would say something like that,' said Tara, which just about clinched it perfectly.

They were sure the plan had worked. Now they just had to give Tara the opportunity to go back to the Year 8 classroom before the rest of them and write on the board. Cassie stormed off in a rehearsed huff and Jasmine followed her, as if to console her. Then Bella pretended she had left her copy of the play they were doing in her dorm and went back to get it, and gradually the others, even those who were not in on the set-up, wandered away to do other things before class started. This, they were pretty sure, would give Tara time to do the deed.

As soon as she left the others, Cassie rushed to Mrs Frost's office. There were only ten minutes before class started and she had to be quick. She met Mrs Frost coming out of the door on her way to a meeting and in her urgency, grabbed hold of her arm, 'You have to come now to the Year 8 classroom and see. It's the only way,' she panted, 'you have to come – we didn't want to do this but it's the only way we'll find out the truth.'

'What is, my dear? Calm down. Now tell me slowly what you're talking about.'

'Can't be slow, no time. Please come to the Year 8 classroom now. I beg you. It's the only way you'll stop thinking badly about me and I can't stand you thinking badly about me. Please!'

She was so urgent and breathless that Mrs Frost agreed to come and Cassie almost dragged her through the corridors and up the stairs.

As soon as they reached the Year 8 classroom, Cassie

flung open the door, praying that it would not all be one huge mistake and the room be empty, but there, standing in front of the board and writing on it, was Tara. When she saw Mrs Frost and Cassie standing in the doorway, she dropped the pen in fright and let out a muted shriek. But she recovered herself almost immediately: her expression altered from one of terror to one of outrage and she pointed indignantly at the board, 'Look at this Mrs Frost. She's done it again.'

They all looked at the writing on the board:

Q: What's the difference between Bella and an elephant?
A: Elepha

And there it stopped.

'I was just trying to rub it off,' said Tara, with a note of trembling desperation in her voice.

She looked Mrs Frost straight in the eye without flinching. Mrs Frost was equally calm. She didn't shout or march over to Tara, she just said quietly, 'Tara, would you bring me the pen you have been writing with.'

'I wasn't writing,' said Tara, her voice getting louder and shakier, 'but here's the pen.' She picked it up. 'Cassie must have dropped it on the floor.'

'I know what I saw, I'm afraid, Tara. I wish I hadn't seen it, believe me. I wish I hadn't seen anyone write something so hurtful. Now, come with me both of you please.'

Mrs Frost called Year 7 and Year 8 together after school that afternoon and told them that Tara had been suspended for the rest of the term and would not therefore be playing Clara in the school production of *The Nutcracker*. She ended with a firm warning:

'She has apologised to the girls concerned and is paying a heavy price for her actions. When she returns next term, I would like you to welcome her warmly with open arms. No reference will ever be made to this incident again. Tara has her troubles, as we all do in our own way, and she deserves your compassion. Accept her for what she is and treat her with love and respect.'

When Princess Octavia asked Cassie to stay behind at the end of the ballet lesson, her heart was racing with excitement and dread. Could it really be what she was hoping for with all her heart? She didn't dare think it in case Princess Octavia was just going to tell her yet again that she looked like a boy and must grow her hair. Cassie hopped from foot to foot and tugged nervously at the edge of her leotard, whilst Princess Octavia waited until all the other girls had left the studio before turning to Cassie. Then, without smiling, she said in a matter-of-fact voice, 'So, you will play Clara now instead of the pretty girl. Pity about your hair but you are the next best dancer.'

Cassie grinned from ear to ear. She almost burst out laughing with delight, but managed to hold it in.

'No need to smile so stupidly. It will be hard work and you will have to be good or the whole performance will fail because of you. Rehearsals continue tomorrow. Anything you would like to ask?'

'No Princess Octavia. Thank you very much. I hope I –'

'Sssh. I'm not interested in what you hope. Off you go.'

Cassie ran straight up to the dorm where Jasmine, Bella and Megan were getting changed out of their uniform. She burst through the door, leapt up onto her bed with a celebratory whoop and jumped up and down in excitement until the bed-springs began to twang dangerously.

'You got the part then?' laughed Bella.

'But how will you manage to catch up?' said Jasmine anxiously. 'You've already missed a week of rehearsals and the performance is only a month away.'

'Don't worry about me,' said Cassie. 'I've seen *The Nutcracker* five million times and I've been dancing the part of Clara in my head for years. I'll work as hard as I have to, to get it right.'

But Jasmine wasn't satisfied.

'I'm going to go through it all with you now,' she said, 'just to make sure you know what's going on. Right,' she went over and sat on Cassie's bed, 'the ballet we're doing has been cut down to three scenes: in the first, it's the Christmas Eve party and the guests are all arriving. Uncle Drosselmeyer gives Clara her present – the soldier nutcracker – but her brother Fritz breaks it, leaving her in floods of tears. This scene ends with a Christmas Eve dance by the whole troupe, and then when they've all gone, Clara dances on her own with the broken nut-cracker soldier, then falls asleep on the sofa. So that's your first solo dance.'

Cassie nodded obediently, smiling sideways at the others.

'In the next scene, she wakes up to see the mouse king attacking her nutcracker who has grown into a life-size prince. Clara throws her slipper at the mouse king who falls over and then she and the nutcracker prince dance together. Got is so far? The final scene is in the kingdom of sweets with all the usual parade of dances – Arabian coffee, Chinese tea and all that – and different groups of girls are doing those. Then there's me as the sugar-plum fairy,' she beamed with pleasure, 'it's perfect for me,' she giggled, 'if I blush, it will look like the sugar-plum fairy is just meant to be pink. Anyway, then you and the prince dance again and you wake up on the sofa with your nutcracker in your hand.'

'Sounds pretty straightforward,' said Cassie, 'so I just have one solo dance and two with the boy who's playing the nutcracker prince. What's he like, by the way?'

'Oh, they've only been shipped in once so far and they were whisked away pretty quickly afterwards. There's Toby and Edward. Toby's Fritz and the prince. He's even quieter than me. In fact, I don't think he's spoken yet. But he looks at us as if he thinks we're just a bunch of annoying little girls.'

Princess Octavia kept Cassie back for extra private lessons over the next two weeks and she had soon learnt the first solo dance. At night, she was exhausted. She almost fell asleep while brushing her teeth and in the mornings had to be shaken awake by the others. But she didn't mind a bit. She even concentrated extra hard in class, determined not to let her schoolwork suffer as a result of the rehearsals. And she couldn't believe it herself when she turned down the offer of a Sunday afternoon trip to the sea so that she could practise instead. The only occasion on which she allowed herself time off was Jasmine's birthday trip to the cinema.

Chapter 10: *A Day Out*

It was Saturday morning and the birds had hardly started singing when Cassie was awoken by an excited Jasmine jumping onto her bed and shaking her.

'Come on, wake up! It's my birthday trip today. We have to get ready. What shall I wear? I can't wait! I still can't believe you did that for me Cassie, especially when I was so disloyal to you, it's so cool of you.'

She had already said this about a thousand times and Cassie had given up telling her it wasn't her fault and she understood. They had got special permission to go into town without a teacher because two of Flo's brothers were going with them and the older one, Gus, was sixteen. Since he had been expelled from his school, he had been hanging around at home and Flo's mum welcomed any opportunity to get him out of the house. At the last minute, Milo had emailed Cassie to ask if he could come and visit her one weekend, so her dad had asked Mrs Frost if he could join the cinema trip as he was like a brother to Cassie. So the whole gang together would be: Cassie, Flo and Jasmine, Milo, Gus and Tom.

'Jasmine!' moaned Cassie, stuffing her head under the pillow, 'it's Saturday – we don't have to be up for ages.

We've got about ten hours until the film starts. I think we can risk staying in bed a bit longer.'

Cassie spent the morning rehearsing with Princess Octavia and then quickly rushed back to the dorm after lunch. She changed into her black jeans and pink leg-warmers, with a baggy black jumper and a purple hat and scarf. Jasmine was agonizing over what to wear and had already changed a hundred times, but eventually she put on her tartan mini-skirt and black leggings with a leather jacket and tartan beret. They met Flo down by the front door and jumped into the cab which was wait-ing to take them to the train station in town where they would meet the boys. The film started at three and they had to be back at school by seven. Four whole hours out of the school grounds unaccompanied – they could hardly believe their luck! Flo texted Gus to say they were on the way and would meet them at the front of the station. Gus texted back saying: 'Just got here. Me, Tom and specky boy.'

'He must mean Milo,' said Cassie, offended. 'He wears glasses – cool little round ones.'

'Oh I never take any notice of anything Gus says,' Flo assured her. 'You'll see why.'

It was starting to get dusky by the time they met the boys at the station. The Christmas lights strung along the lamp-posts on the high street were glowing orange against the charcoal sky. Milo had got on the train with the other two in London and he and Tom had already made friends, but

Gus was striding ahead, trying not to be with them. Gus was a huge boy with a loud honking voice, who burped a lot and seemed always to be pushing someone, although it was somehow disguised as friendliness. Cassie could easily see why Flo was so against brothers, and boys in general. As soon as he saw the girls he yelled out, 'Hey Flo – over here! What have you done to your hair? It looks like an elephant sat on it.'

Flo, who had tried to use straighteners on her mad frizzy hair, raised her eyes at Cassie and said, 'See? This is what I have to put up with all the time. You're so lucky not to have any.'

Gus was annoyed about having to go to the cinema with a 'bunch of shrimps' and made up for it by teasing and embarrassing them all. There was a man selling roasted chestnuts in paper cones outside the station and Gus said loudly,

'Acorns? We're not squirrels, why would we want to eat acorns?'

Then he carried on talking loudly and rudely about everyone around them, so the others hurried on ahead to the cinema and pretended they weren't with him.

After saying a quick 'Hi' to Cassie, Milo had carried on talking to Tom about football and bikes and they had both pretty much ignored the girls.

At the cinema, the girls bought a huge bucket of popcorn to share and a drink each, Tom and Milo both got hotdogs and Gus got a huge bucket of popcorn to himself and a packet of bubblegum. While they were waiting for the film to start, Gus threw popcorn over at the girls and blew huge pink bubbles which popped all over his face. Then, five minutes after the film started he suddenly got up and said,

'This is rubbish! Strictly for five-year olds. I'm off.' And he left the cinema.

'Phew!' Jasmine whispered to Cassie. 'Now we can enjoy the film.'

When they came out of the cinema it was properly dark and beginning to get frosty. Much to their disappointment, Gus was waiting for them outside.

'We've still got two hours 'til we have to be back at school,' said Cassie. 'What shall we do?'

'How exciting!' said Jasmine. 'We can do whatever we like – like proper grown-ups.'

'Oooh like proper grown-ups,' squealed Gus, imitating her voice, 'not!'

'Oh shut up!' said Tom, 'can't you go off and do something else?'

'Let's go to a café for hot chocolate,' said Flo, and everyone agreed.

They could see a cafe further up the high street, close to the river, and they headed in that direction.

'What the hell are you wearing?' said Gus, tugging at Flo's precious feather boa. 'You look like an old loony granny.'

'Leave it alone! I've been wearing your old jeans and jumpers all my life and I'm fed up with it. I want to be glamorous, that's all.'

But before she had even finished speaking, Gus grabbed the end of her feather boa and flicked it so suddenly that it slid off her neck. Flo tried to reach out for it but Gus held it up higher than she could stretch and laughed.

'Hey, give it back to her,' said Milo quietly.

'Go on Gus, leave her alone,' said Tom giving him a shove.

But it made no difference, Gus just twirled it around in the air above their heads, saying in a loud whiny voice,

'Oh no, she's not a glamorous pwintheth any more.'

Flo finally managed to grab hold of one end of her boa but Gus pulled it back so sharply that it broke in two and pink feathers fluttered down to the ground. Flo yelped like a kicked puppy.

'My feather boa! Oh, Gus I hate you, I hate you!'

She wasn't quite crying but only because she was making a supreme effort not to. She thumped her brother with both fists as hard as she could, but although he stopped laughing, he didn't apologise. He just said dismissively, 'I'm sure you can sew it back together or something.'

They were at the coffee shop by now, its tinselly windows glowing with warmth. Inside, the tables were crowded with people clasping steaming mugs.

'Oh, just go away!' said Flo miserably.

'Happy to,' said Gus. 'Rather not come to your dollies' tea-party anyway. See you back at the station, Tom,' and he walked off towards the river.

'Thank god for that,' said Milo. Then he turned to Flo,

112

'Look, I'm sure you can fix it. Or I could buy you another one if you like. My mum would know where to get one.'

'Thanks,' said Flo, flushing with pleasure and suddenly cheering up. 'I probably can fix it, you're right.'

They went into the coffee shop and sat at a table in the window. They all ordered huge cups of hot chocolate with fluffy marshmallows floating on top, and Milo bought them each a red and white striped sugar cane.

They sat there sucking their candy sticks and talking about their different schools. The girls told Tom and Milo all about the dramas at Starlight Academy over the white-board messages, then about Cassie getting the part of Clara in *The Nutcracker* at the last minute.

'You're doing a play about a nutcracker? That sounds interesting,' said Tom sarcastically.

'Not a play, a ballet you idiot,' said Flo, 'haven't you even heard of it?'

'Anyway, you probably wouldn't be interested unless it was called *The Cricketer*,' said Cassie.

Tom laughed.

'Yeah – but I still wouldn't watch it if it was a ballet,' he said.

'I can't really imagine a ballet about a cricketer somehow,' said Jasmine, and then blushed and looked like she wished she hadn't spoken.

'We're doing a rap at my school. It's called Three Blind Lice. One of the girls in Year 10 wrote it. About some headlice on someone's head – like, their view of life or something.'

'Wow, that sounds so interesting and original,' said Flo, 'are you in it?'

'No way,' said Milo, 'I hate that kind of thing. It's so trying to be cool.'

'Is it? Oh,' said Flo.

It seemed like they had hardly been in there any time at all when suddenly Flo yelped, 'Oh my golly gosh, it's nearly six thirty. We have to be back in half an hour.'

She jumped up and her chair clattered backwards into the table behind them.

'Did you really just say golly gosh?' laughed Milo.

'What's wrong with that?' asked Flo, frowning defensively.

'Nothing really I suppose, it's quite sweet actually.'

'It's not *sweet*! I just don't like saying *oh my god*, that's all. I think it's kind of rude. Anyway, come on you lot, we have to get back.'

'Flo likes her rules,' explained Cassie.

'I know,' said Tom smiling, 'she's always writing lists of rules at home and sticking them on the fridge but somehow we always accidentally spill stuff on them.'

They left the coffee shop and walked back to the station, where the girls got a cab back to school and the boys waited to meet up with Gus for the train back to London.

'That was my best birthday ever,' said Jasmine sleepily as they snuggled down into their duvets that night. 'Just the best.'

Chapter 11: *Rehearsals Begin*

On Sunday afternoon, Cassie had another rehearsal with Princess Octavia, only this time the boy who was playing both Fritz and the nutcracker prince would be rehearsing with them. Princess Octavia had instructed her not to do anything 'tiresome' that morning, so after breakfast, they spent a lazy morning reading magazines and chatting in the Common Room and then went for a slow, meandering bike ride before lunch.

'I had the weirdest dream last night,' said Flo as they were weaving about on their bikes in the pale winter sunshine.

'Oh no, not a weird dream! *Please* don't tell us about it,' begged Cassie, 'other people's weird dreams are always so boring.'

'This is a really quick one though,' said Flo. 'I was swimming in a cup of hot chocolate using marshmallows as floats when suddenly I started drowning, and your friend Milo held out a candy cane to rescue me. Isn't that weird?'

Cassie and Jasmine laughed.

'Not so weird,' said Jasmine. 'I dreamt I was doing the dance of the sugar-plum fairy but when I looked down at my feet they were yellow flippers, then I looked in a mirror and I was a penguin, but a sort of sugar-plum penguin with sugar-plum earrings.'

'I must have been too tired to dream last night, otherwise I'd bore you with mine,' said Cassie. 'I swear I've never worked so hard in my life. Every single muscle in my body aches, but kind of in a good way.'

Princess Octavia was hunched on her stool in a corner looking miserable when Cassie turned up for her afternoon rehearsal. She often looked miserable, so that was nothing new, but usually she managed to say something insulting, whereas today she was completely silent. Cassie dropped to the floor and tied on her shoes, then she went over to the *barre* and began to do some stretches. She knew better than to disturb Princess Octavia without good reason.

'You are a good girl Cassie,' came a quiet voice from the corner.

Cassie was so shocked, not only by the weak voice, but by the fact that she had spoken her name – by the fact that she even *knew* her name – that she straightened up and looked at Princess Octavia, waiting for her to say something else.

'I was once like you. I was thinking while I waited for you, how like you I once was.'

Cassie tried to picture Princess Octavia being like her but she couldn't. The lined, bony face, as of an angel in an old painting, and the wispy silver hair, were too far away from whatever it was that she had once been.

'I was not like the other girls. I loved dancing but I did

not love the things that other girls loved – pink ribbons and ponies and jewels, that sort of thing.'

Cassie was thrilled to hear Princess Octavia talking like this and desperate for her to go on, but at that moment, Toby the Royal Ballet boy turned up. He came in apologising for his lateness, and Princess Octavia turned abruptly from Cassie to say, 'And what if the nutcracker prince really had been late, ha? He would have missed Christmas Eve altogether and no ballet.'

Princess Octavia took them through fifteen minutes of warm-up exercises at the *barre* and then they practised some key movements in the middle of the room. Toby was a brilliant dancer but not very friendly. He hardly looked at Cassie, though not in a shy way; she could tell he just didn't think she was worth the effort. He, after all, was at the Royal Ballet School and he would have seen Starlight Academy girls as childish amateurs. He did exactly what he had to do, and partnered Cassie perfectly, lifting her up into the air with ease, but he was so cold. Cassie had looked forward to dancing with a boy properly for the first time, just to see what it would be like, but she was disappointed. She didn't feel like she was dancing with him so much as being his prop.

They started with the scene when the guests arrive and Clara and Fritz peek through the banisters to see them in all their finery. In this scene, they were supposed to be jostling with each other to see more clearly. They were miming:

Let *me* see!

No, let *me*!

Your head's so big I can't see anything.

Well, your elbows are so sharp you keep poking my ribs.

Cassie quite enjoyed this scene because she found Toby so annoying already, and she elbowed him out of the way a little too enthusiastically.

'Princess Octavia,' he protested, 'this girl's being far too rough. She's meant to be playing a young girl, not some hefty sumo wrestler.'

'Huh!' said Cassie irritably.

'Try to bear it like a man, Toby, I'm sure she won't hurt you too badly' said Princess Octavia impatiently. 'And the girl's name is Cassie,' she added.

After that, they hardly looked at each other, which suited the part perfectly. Next, they had to be startled by the entrance of Uncle Drosselmeyer, who sweeps in through the door in a black cloak, gives Fritz his toy soldiers and Clara her nutcracker. When Fritz tries to crack a large nut, it breaks and he flings it angrily aside. As all of this was going on, Cassie was getting crosser and crosser with Toby, more than she was with Fritz. Her dance alone at midnight, when everyone else is in bed, they saved for later, and moved straight on to Clara's first dance with the nutcracker prince after they have beaten the mouse king together. Princess Octavia had choreographed this herself and she and Cassie had been practising the triumphant *pas de chat*, springing like a cat, on which it was largely based, for days. But no sooner had they begun than Toby raised his hand to stop the music and asked Princess Octavia with a puzzled look on his face, 'I'm sorry, but has she learnt the *pas de chat* yet?'

'Yes she has!' huffed Cassie hotly.

'Oh,' said Toby breezily, 'I wasn't sure.'

After that, Cassie couldn't get anything right. She felt Toby criticising her even when he didn't say anything, and all her moves seemed clumsy and ugly.

Towards the end of the rehearsal, they began practising the most difficult move in the whole dance. Cassie stood with her back to Toby and he lifted her up in the air with his hands clasped around her waist. She had one knee bent up and the other fell along the length of his leg as she leant back against his body. They had practised this sequence over and over again and Toby was just about to start spinning her around in that position when he suddenly spluttered and coughed and put her down with a thud.

'Princess Octavia!' he shouted, as if he was telling her off, 'her hair keeps getting in my mouth. Can't you make her do something about it?'

Cassie was embarrassed and tried desperately to smooth her hair down but it kept springing up wilfully. She thought of Tara and her fine strands of golden hair swept slickly back into a perfectly tight bun. Well, she wasn't like Tara! And he would just have to get used to it.

Princess Octavia merely shook her head and sighed impatiently, 'Little boy, stop coughing. You sound like a cat with a hair-ball.'

After that, it went from bad to worse. Cassie made a complete mess of a *grande jeté*, even though she had been practising it for weeks. She was so terrified of getting it wrong that when Toby put his hands around her waist to lift her up for the leap, she froze and stood rigid on the ground, so that instead of launching her off into the air, he ended up squeezing her waist painfully.

'Ouch!' Cassie couldn't help yelling.

'Princess Octavia!' Toby whined in complaint. 'Isn't there anyone else who could take this part? I find it really difficult to dance with her. She'll be fine in a few years, I'm sure, but at the moment ...'

Princess Octavia only laughed and instructed them to start again from the beginning.

I bet he wouldn't complain about Tara, Cassie thought to herself miserably as she prepared herself to give it another go.

After the rehearsal, Cassie stayed behind to talk to Princess Octavia. Not only was her body more tired than it had ever been before, but her heart felt like a withered balloon.

'Am I really as bad as he makes out?' she asked her teacher hopelessly.

'You still need much practice certainly,' replied the princess, 'but you will get there. You have a natural sense of movement and your body is well-trained from the beginning, so it is more likely you will succeed. Keep working. These boys – puffed up like pastry! They think they are rare sweet delicacies.'

Princess Octavia seemed in such a friendly mood that Cassie dared tentatively to ask her another question – the one she had been longing to ask all afternoon.

'So why did it make you sad? To think about how you were once like me.'

'It always makes an old person sad to think of the young person buried forever inside them. Besides, I was like you once, but you will fulfil your potential one day and I never did.'

'But you taught Margot Fonteyn.'

'No. Never did. Only read her book.'

She said it in such a matter-of-fact way that Cassie wasn't even shocked.

'Oh, I was a brilliant dancer once,' Princess Octavia went on, 'but just as I was about to take over as principal ballerina at the Kirov, the Germans besieged our city. It was 1941. I was sixteen-years old. My family – we had to flee our homeland. For many years we lived in hiding, because my father had been an important man and there were people searching for him. And when finally we settled in England, it was too late for me. Although I had practised every day that I could, even when we were squeezed altogether in a coal cellar for many weeks, I was twenty one and had had no formal tuition for five years. There was no hope for me. My father had died of pneumonia in the last year of our captivity, and my elder brother had been shot. When we arrived in England, my mother, my sister and I had to work to survive. My sister had been a talented musician, but she never picked up a violin again. It was too painful for her. When I met Lady Anthea Price, she had just founded Starlight Academy, and she took me on as a teacher here. It was the best I could hope for, and she became like a second mother to me.'

Cassie was so awestruck that she did not know what to say. What *could* she say? It was as if she had just met an entirely new person, and she was so full of deep admiration that there was nothing she could say to express it. She would never in a million years understand what it was like to be Princess Octavia. To think of what she had been through, how she had suffered and how hard she had worked, just to keep dancing, made her feel ashamed. Everything had always been handed to Cassie on a plate. Her dad had enrolled her in dancing lessons as a child, she had been good, it had been quite easy, and she had never faced any difficulties. She loved dancing, but she didn't know if she loved it as much as Princess Octavia did. She didn't know if she could practise it in a damp, dark, freezing coal cellar. Suddenly, a spark of determination fired up inside her, and with it a surge of love for the cranky old Princess. Without thinking about it, she rushed over and hugged her tight, and to her surprise Princess Octavia put her arms around her.

'I am not even a real princess,' she said sadly, almost with a sob.

'What do you mean?'

'Well, I am in name, but in name only. Not on the inside. Not a princess on the inside any more.'

She suddenly shrugged Cassie off brusquely.

'Enough of this nonsense. Time for you to go. I want to see you early tomorrow, before the start of lessons.'

Chapter 12: *First Night*

Despite feeling increasingly exhausted, Cassie worked harder and harder. She set her alarm so that she could get up an hour earlier and, pulling on her legwarmers in the dark and grabbing a banana to eat on the way, rushed to the studio to practise before breakfast. She practised hundreds of *battements* and *rondes de jambe* in an effort to strengthen her leg muscles and improve her technique. After morning lessons, there were rehearsals all afternoon, and then after dinner and prep, she usually met Princess Octavia for private rehearsals until bed-time. As a result, Cassie hardly saw her friends at all, apart from Jasmine, with whom she shared some rehearsal time.

The Nutcracker was due to be performed on the last day of term. In the final week leading up to the show, the teachers gave up on lessons altogether and the entire timetable was given over to the performance. Those not involved on stage – that is, the singers and actors – were busy with posters, scenery, sound, lighting, or ticket sales. Cassie had managed to miss most of the end-of-term Christmas fun, but on the final Wednesday, Bella organized a Gingerbread Teacher competition and Cassie allowed herself a couple of hours off so that she could join in. The competition was a secret from the teachers, who thought Bella needed extra help designing and producing *The Nutcracker* programmes and so let the whole of Years 7 and 8, thirty girls altogether, take over the art room for the afternoon.

Instead, Bella had convinced one of the school cooks to make a huge batch of gingerbread men ('as a surprise for the teachers') and then had persuaded her mum to send her a massive collection of coloured icing tubes along with loads of assorted cake decorating bits and pieces. Once the door was closed, she explained the rules of the competition.

'No one must breathe a *word* about who their Gingerbread Teacher is meant to be,' she said in a dramatically serious voice, as if they were at a top-secret spy conference instead of in the art room on a Wednesday afternoon with a load of gingerbread men.

'You have exactly one hour to make your Gingerbread Teacher,' she continued with increasing seriousness, and then added, 'because then we've *really* got to get on with making these programmes.'

They talked and laughed happily as they iced faces and hairstyles onto their gingerbread people and improvised clothes with the cake decorations. At the end of the session, Bella collected in all of the Gingerbread Teachers and held each one up for inspection. By the time she had finished, they were all aching with laughter and everyone voted for the winner, writing their nomination on a scrap of paper and putting it in a Christmas stocking. After Bella had counted the votes, Jasmine was announced as the winner with her perfect gingerbread version of Mr Broccoli, who had very realistic green florets of broccoli in place of his curly hair. Next, Bella laid all the Gingerbread Teachers out on cardboard trays and displayed them in the school reception, then printed off a memo to each teacher saying: *'Please come and collect your gingerbread twin who is waiting for you in reception.'* It was the kind of stunt that only Bella dared attempt, and only she could pull off. She was so good at making the teachers laugh, that they usually forgave her practical jokes.

On Thursday morning, Cassie had a final rehearsal with Toby before the whole-cast dress rehearsal on Thursday evening. She had woken up feeling sick and though she didn't want to eat at all, had forced down half a bowl of cereal at breakfast. Her heart was racing and she couldn't stop tapping her feet under the table in a way that annoyed even her. Whenever anyone talked to her, she wished they wouldn't. In fact, she wanted nothing more than to run off into the woods and climb up a tree and never come down. Flo came to sit next to her at breakfast and squeezed her arm affectionately.

'So, one day to go. Can't wait!'

'Oh don't say that. I'm trying really hard not to think about it.'

Cassie had been thinking very deliberately all morning about Christmas: about eating chocolate in bed, and opening her stocking with her dad by the fire, and going next door to Milo's house for games, and then to her grandparents for Christmas dinner, and sledging with the family who lived next door to her grandparents, then more games by the fire in the evening. But she couldn't ignore the fact that a huge gaping hole lay between now and Christmas, just waiting to swallow her up. If only she could avoid it somehow! But she couldn't. There was no way around it. She had to get through the performance somehow. And the more she tried to ignore the hole, the bigger and blacker it got.

'You're going to be brilliant,' said Flo, squeezing her even more tightly. 'Trust me. They'll probably snap you up for the Royal Ballet and you'll have to leave us, and we'll be all sad, and everyone will be like, why didn't we recognise how great she was when she was here, and now she's gone ...'

'OK, OK, I get the message,' said Cassie, smiling weakly, 'and thanks, but actually it doesn't help. I still feel rubbish.'

'Huh! This reminds me of our first meal here together – you all miserable and rude, and me trying my best to be nice to you because I felt sorry for you.'

Cassie laughed again, 'Thanks a lot! I thought you really liked me.'

'No. I just felt sorry for you because you hadn't dressed up all grandly like me. Anyway, I'm sure Tom's looking forward to it, even if you're not.'

'Tom's coming?' said Cassie, trying not to sound as alarmed as she felt.

'Yup. Poor thing. He's begged Mum not to make him come – can't think of anything worse, he says – but she says she needs someone to map-read for her. I'm glad really because she's quite likely to end up in Scotland otherwise. She never can remember where Starlight Academy is.'

'Great,' said Cassie with a mournful sigh, 'so that's one member of the audience who definitely doesn't want to be here. I wonder how many others there will be.'

'Oh, I didn't mean you to take it that way. It's only Tom anyway – who cares what he thinks? Besides, he'll probably be plugged into his iPod, so he might not even notice the ballet.'

When she walked into the dance studio after breakfast, Cassie was surprised to be greeted by a smile from Toby. She nearly fell over and looked behind her just to check it was her he was smiling at.

'How are you this morning?' asked Princess Octavia.

'I feel like crying and I want to go home,' said Cassie truthfully.

Toby laughed.

'If it makes you feel any better, I feel pretty much the same.'

'*You* do?'

Cassie had assumed he would only be thinking about how grateful everyone in the audience would be to see him dance. And then she realised, 'Oh, you mean you're worried I'm going to mess it up for you? Well don't worry –'

'No, I didn't mean that,' he cut in, looking a bit embarrassed. 'Sorry, have I been that rude? Actually I think you've got loads better just in the last couple of weeks. It's amazing really.'

Cassie flushed with pleasure. She was surprised to feel quite so pleased, given how she felt about Toby, but his hard-won praise was just the encouragement she needed.

It was Friday afternoon. The performance was due to start in three hours and the corridors were full of excitement as girls charged to and fro, delivering costumes, rushing to make-up, and practising lines. Miss Chivers was putting the finishing touches to the set and Mr Broccoli was running through the light sequence. The dancers had a couple of hours off before they had to start warming up for the performance and Toby was looking around nervously.

'So, what shall we do?' he wondered. 'I mean I have to hang about and I don't really have anywhere to hang about.'

'I thought you lot were being strictly monitored,' said Cassie. 'I thought they sort of locked you in a cupboard or something in between rehearsals.'

'Well it's not quite that bad,' he laughed, 'but I guess they are pretty precious about us – try to keep us out of harm's way.'

'How awful,' said Cassie. And then she had a thought. 'I know. Why don't we go down to the woods? I go there whenever I get a chance, although they're quite strict with us here too.'

'Sounds great,' said Toby. He was like a different boy. She couldn't believe how friendly he was being.

On the way down to the woods, Cassie told him about her favourite tree, and how she had once climbed up it and got stuck and made her and Flo late for a lesson.

'Boy, there was trouble,' she said, shaking her head in recollection. 'You'd have thought we tried to burn the school down the way they reacted.'

'I don't think I've ever climbed a tree,' said Toby.

'Never climbed a tree?' said Cassie in disbelief. 'What have you been doing all your life then?'

'Dancing of course, you idiot.'

'Oh yeah, I suppose. And anyway, how come you're so nice now and before you were so dreadful?'

'Was I that bad? Sorry. But, to be fair, you were a pretty terrible dancer a few weeks ago.'

'Hey! I was not!'

'I can't help it really,' he began to explain. 'You know, for me dancing is a serious thing, the most important thing in my life. I can't afford to make mistakes. And obviously I don't want to look a fool. So if I think I'm going to be dancing with someone sub-standard, I make a bit of a fuss about it. To protect my future, my career. It's not just fun for me, you know.'

'No, I can see that,' said Cassie. She thought that any moment she was going to start disliking him again, but then he smiled.

'I must seem a bit of an idiot at times,' he shrugged, 'but to be honest I don't mind if people think that about me. I only mind about dancing.'

She couldn't help but admire him somehow, for his dedication and determination, even if he was a bit annoying.

They had reached the tree by now and Cassie pointed up the tree trunk, 'You first then. I feel immensely privileged that I'm going to witness your first-ever tree climb.'

'Don't be stupid – I'm not going up,' said Toby.

'Why on earth not? You're not frightened are you?'

'Of course not, but three hours before a performance? You must be mad. Why would I take that risk?'

Cassie just didn't get him.

'What, the risk of being kidnapped by a squirrel?'

'The risk of falling, you idiot. And you can make me feel as chicken as you like, I'm not going up and I couldn't care less what you think of me.'

'OK then,' said Cassie, as she began to climb the tree, 'I'll just have to throw some chocolate down to you. I've got a whole stash in a hole up there.'

'It's a great view from up here, you should really try it,' she yelled down to him, but he just laughed.

'Get on with it and throw the chocolate down.'

They had an odd sort of conversation, with Cassie up a tree and Toby firmly on the ground, but she was beginning to like him more and more.

'Come on, it's time to go,' he said eventually.

'Oh sorry, I can't come down. My hair's caught in a branch.'

He threw a stick up at her.

'OK, I'm off. I'm sure we'll easily find someone else to replace you,' and he strode off back to the school, leaving Cassie to clamber down in a hurry and run after him, just in case he wasn't joking.

Standing in the wings, Cassie could see the edges of her tutu fluttering with nerves. Her legs were trembling so much that she couldn't imagine being able to walk on, let alone dance. She dropped a few *plies* in an attempt to push the nerves away but it was no use. The orchestra was tuning up – there were lines of notes running up and down here, there and everywhere – and suddenly she heard Flo's flute sing out. She just knew it was Flo's by the way she played it – just like an over-excited baby bird. The thought of Flo sitting down there comforted her. So it *wasn't* just her. There was Flo, too. And now as she looked around she could see Jasmine doing nervous little jumps in the wings at the other side of the stage. And behind her, Princess Octavia, who was hunched on her stool, tapping her cane on the floor and frowning at the tip of it. But she straightened up and smiled when she saw Cassie look over at her. So it wasn't just her. It was everyone. This performance was not about her. It was about all of them, and the audience, and the musicians, and the man who wrote the ballet in the first place, and all the dancers who had ever danced it. She felt something float up off her chest and the orchestra struck up the first bars of the overture.

And then it was all over. In what seemed a single breath, it was over. Cassie had enjoyed her dances so much that she wished they would never end, but all too soon they were on the final scene and then the audience was beginning to clap and it was all over. As she stepped forward with Toby to curtsey, the applause seemed to whisk her off the ground, as if she was floating up high on the string of a helium balloon. She tried desperately to hold herself down, to hold on to something on the ground and stop herself floating away altogether out of sight, but she couldn't. She couldn't help herself being carried off on a wave of complete and utter happiness. She could see her dad in the audience, clapping madly, smiling from ear to ear, even putting a cupped hand to his mouth and whooping. Cassie almost burst out laughing – it was so unlike him to whoop, he was normally so quiet and reserved. And then just as quickly, that was all over too. The curtain fell and the string of her balloon was cut, and she landed on the ground with a thud. She joined in all the excitement along with the others, and hugged everyone and giggled helplessly as they tripped all over the place trying to get out of their costumes in a hurry, but her heart wasn't really in it. The light inside her had gone out. She rushed over to Toby to say well done, but he looked grumpy and shrugged, 'It wasn't exactly my best. You were OK mostly, but there were a few times when you made it really difficult.'

Toby's spiky comment didn't hurt her as much as it might once have done. It was just the way he was, and he couldn't help it, just as she couldn't help the way she was. Somehow, the wave of excitement all around her was enough to carry Cassie through without her bursting out crying, which was what she felt like doing deep down inside. She found Flo as quickly as she could and they linked arms back-to-back and side-skipped along the corridors together to find their families. Cassie tried to wipe the thick greasy make-up off her face as she went, and tried to ruffle some of the hair-spray out of her stiff hair, but by the time they reached the hall she still looked like an electrocuted, melting clown.

'I can't believe this is it,' Flo said breathlessly as they skipped into the dining hall where the parents were making their usual racket.

'I know – the end of our first term. I can't believe it's only been one term. It seems like a lifetime.'

'And it's going to be a lifetime until we see each other again,' said Flo mournfully. 'Three whole weeks. And nothing to look forward to but snowballs in the face and whoopee cushions every time I sit down. Yippee!' she said miserably, 'Three weeks with my stinky brothers.'

The hall was full of parents laughing and chinking glasses. Cassie found her dad standing by Flo's mum and another man she did not recognise.

'Dad!' screamed Flo in delight, and rushed into his arms.

Flo's dad, who was a deep-sea diver kind of scientist, spent most of his time underwater and didn't see much of his family, but he had just flown back from South America as a surprise, and Flo couldn't have been happier. Cassie ran up to her own dad and he lifted her up in the air and spun her around as if she was three years old, but for once she didn't mind. Flo's brother Tom was there with his hands in his pockets, shuffling and frowning and looking around for an escape route. Cassie's dad carried on his conversation with Flo's dad about the political situation in Chile, and Flo's mum went off to find the glass she had put down somewhere, and Flo ran off to find Jasmine, and once again Cassie was left standing silently next to Tom. He stopped shuffling and looked around nervously for a moment to check no one was near, and then said quite quickly in a low voice, 'I'm not into ballet or anything but I thought you were quite good.'

Cassie's face glowed and she felt that she would burst with happiness, but before she could answer her dad leant over to her, 'We've been invited to the Logans' New Years Eve party. We're not doing anything, are we?'

'No,' Cassie replied without pausing for thought. Flo had come back in time to hear and she gave Cassie a massive hug,

'So it will only be *half* a lifetime after all.'

'And I'm really looking forward to all those whoopee cushions and snowballs,' grinned Cassie.

Acknowledgements

Pamela Shirley and Martin West at Ragged Bears, who have made this happen

Susie, for first suggesting the idea and for all her support

Marion, for lending me all her friends

Simon Walter and Martin Couzins, for generous technological help

The Walter girls of Camberley and the Spratt girls of Dublin, my first readers

Mark for his constant love and loyalty

Look out for Book 2 in the Starlight Academy series

DOUBLE DRAMA
AT STARLIGHT ACADEMY

At the start of Spring Term Cassie and Flo are looking
forward to new adventures at **Starlight Academy** –
their fun loving friend Bella had landed the star role in
the school production of *As You Like It*, and Cassie has
started up a Wilderness Club in the woods.

But things start to go wrong when a new teacher arrives
and Bella's sense of fun gets her into trouble. In the
end, the friends have to take drastic action to put it all
right, but will they get away with it?